Readers love the R
by M.J. O'

Coming Home

"This is a nice and comfortable story."
—Elisa - My Reviews and Ramblings

"This was a good, solid read… If you are a fan of rocky love stories, characters learning who they are and being true to themselves… then I recommend you grab a copy of this one."
—MM Good Book Reviews

Letting Go

"I liked the writing style and I found the story comfortable and enjoyable. It's a nice, easy read that left me feeling happy. I liked it."
—Reviews by Jessewave

Finding Shelter

"*Finding Shelter* left me feeling warm and happy."
—Live Your Life, Buy the Book

"From the moment I picked up *Finding Shelter* I knew I was on to a winner… It's a book I know I could pick up to read again and again when I just want something to make me feel good!"
—Love Bytes

"I so loved this story for everything it was: sweet, romantic, touching, and uplifting."
—The Novel Approach

By M.J. O'Shea

Catch My Breath
Cross Bones (Dreamspinner Anthology)
Corkscrewed
With Anna Martin: Macarons at Midnight
Newton's Laws of Attraction • Impractical Magic
Stroke!

LUCKY MOON SERIES (WITH PIPER VAUGHN)
Moonlight Becomes You
The Luckiest

ROCK BAY SERIES
Coming Home
Letting Go
Finding Shelter

ONE THING SERIES (WITH PIPER VAUGHN)
One Small Thing
One True Thing

Published by DREAMSPINNER PRESS
http://www.dreamspinnerpress.com

CORKSCREWED
M.J. O'SHEA

Dreamspinner Press

Published by
DREAMSPINNER PRESS

5032 Capital Circle SW, Suite 2, PMB# 279, Tallahassee, FL 32305-7886   USA
http://www.dreamspinnerpress.com/

This is a work of fiction. Names, characters, places, and incidents either are the product of author imagination or are used fictitiously, and any resemblance to actual persons, living or dead, business establishments, events, or locales is entirely coincidental.

Corkscrewed
© 2014 M.J. O'Shea.

Cover Art
© 2014 L.C. Chase.
www.lcchase.com
Cover content is for illustrative purposes only and any person depicted on the cover is a model.

ISBN: 978-1-63216-525-1
Digital ISBN: 978-1-63216-526-8
Library of Congress Control Number: 2014947597
First Edition December 2014

Printed in the United States of America
∞
This paper meets the requirements of
ANSI/NISO Z39.48-1992 (Permanence of Paper).

CHAPTER 1

San Francisco

HE LOOKED at the only person he'd ever trusted, the only one who'd been there for him, who'd taught him how to do more than merely survive, helped him become something other than a dirty street kid with no home and no future. Roman. His friend. His mentor. His only family.

Roman was leaving.

"You're gonna be fine, kid. I promise. I've got ya set up for life if you pull off this one last job."

That didn't help. At all. Thick and suffocating panic rushed him hard at the thought of being alone. Truly and forever alone. He thought he might pass out. He couldn't do it by himself. He'd never even tried. Roman had been there since the beginning, since he'd pulled him, dirty and skinny and always half a step away from jail or death, off the streets back when he was a kid. He needed Roman. He was nothing without him.

"I don't want to do this alone. Let me come with you."

His mentor shook his head. "That's not your road, kid. If you pull this off, you won't have to hide. You'll have whatever you want. More money than you know what to do with."

"But you're my family." He sounded like a baby, he knew he did, but the thought of being alone again after years of having someone who cared was daunting at best, terrifying at worst. He'd never done well trying to survive on his own. "I want to come with you. We can come back when the heat is off."

"They've got too much on me, kid. I won't be coming back."

He sighed. There was no arguing with Roman. They were both stubborn, but they also knew who'd win in the end. "What do I need to do?"

A newspaper landed on the table, loud in the silence of their shared loft, creased and yellowed, with a date ten years old. There was a boy splashed on the front page: thirteen, maybe fifteen tops, with huge blue eyes, inky black waves of hair, pale skin, expensive clothes, happy grin.

He gasped.

"Who is that? He looks like... me. Exactly like me." It was hard not to touch, to reach out and test the curve of familiar eyes, perfectly positioned dimples, even the right tilt to his smile. He barely remembered his face at that age. Mostly it had been covered with a thick layer of dirt and grime. He didn't remember much of anything before it, nothing, really, just flashes of the street and fear and cold. He stared for a long time.

"He's been missing since three days before this newspaper came out."

"Wait. Do you think this boy is me?"

"I think this kid was an only child with a huge trust fund, a loving step-grandmother who'd do anything to have her baby back, and no living biological family. Other than that...." Roman shrugged. "You do the math. You don't remember your childhood before your teens, this boy disappeared when he was a teen from the scene of a car crash that killed his parents. You look like twins. Kid, you couldn't ask for a better setup."

"What are you trying to say?" He was usually so quick to pick up the plan, but the boy's familiar smiling face had jarred him.

"I'm saying this is yours. This is your future. All you have to do is walk in there and convince them you're the missing Isaac Shelley, and then you are."

He couldn't believe what Roman was proposing. "So I'm Anastasia. Is that what you're saying? I'm the lost heir. It's the oldest con in the book. They'd have to be stupid to believe me. Nobody's going to buy that."

"Nobody has to except for Marigold Shelley. It might be the oldest con in the book but how many people out there have your face? If the grandmother signs over Isaac Shelley's trust account, that's all you need. You can do this."

"So this is about getting some dead kid's trust fund? That'll make up for the fact that the only family I have is walking out the door?"

Roman clapped him gently on the shoulder. "My son, you need to decide what you want out of it in the end. I'm just handing you the vehicle. It's up to you to drive it."

"You're really not going to come back ever?" Just saying the words hurt. One jagged stab wound at a time. He felt like a child, crying when his parent left for the night. But it wasn't one night, and even if he was twenty-four years old, he wanted to cry. The thought of years gaping black and empty, alone, made his heart race and his palms sweat.

Roman shook his head. "I can't, son. I've been burned. Too many agents with too many very official letters on their badges are after me. My aliases are toast. As soon as they find my accounts, they'll freeze them. I need to get out of the country."

Too many agents after him… burned aliases. A wanted man. It couldn't be.

"You aren't—" He couldn't finish the sentence. He almost didn't want to know.

"The Black Mamba?" Roman chuckled. "I'm surprised it took you this long to ask. I'm not. I met her once on a job, then ran into her a few months back in Miami when you were pulling that job in Denver. Turns out she doesn't like to be crossed."

"Wait. The Black Mamba is a woman?"

"She's exactly what her name says she is. A snake."

"And she screwed you over."

"She didn't want me messing with another one of her precious prizes." Roman shrugged, curiously unfazed, like it was all part of the game. Perhaps it was.

"Where is she now?"

"I don't know. Hopefully far away from me. Don't go looking for something you don't want to find, son."

There was something off about Roman's voice. He didn't think anyone else would pick it up, but he knew his mentor well. He nodded. It was really over. Roman was leaving. "How do I stay in touch with you?"

Roman was by the door, bag slung over his shoulder. "You don't, kid. Good luck."

And then the door closed and Roman was gone.

Two months later….

SONOMA COUNTY was pretty, in a bucolic, hazy sort of way, rolling green hills covered with neat rows of grape vines and grass so gold and waving, Van Gogh would've been envious of its color. Yeah, the place was beautiful. If you liked that kind of thing. Cary Talbot didn't. He figured if he were anyone else, he'd find himself charmed by the roll of the hills and the dusty golden glow. But he wasn't charmed. He was lost. Totally, completely, fuck-if-he-had-a-clue lost. He'd been winding around picturesque country roads for hours, his GPS was having some sort of meltdown, and he was on the verge of pulling to the side of the road and throwing the damn thing as far as he could. Because, you know. That would help.

He took another turn that the angry lady in the computer told him to take, which landed him in some sort of roundabout that led absofuckinglutely nowhere.

"Recalculating… recalculating."

"Screw you!" He slammed his hand on the steering wheel. "Ow, fuck." He was lost, and his hand hurt like hell.

"Turn left in thirty feet. Turn left…. Turn left." The voice got more insistent, but it didn't change the facts.

"There is no damn left turn here!"

"Recalculating…." Of course that's when the car's Bluetooth picked up his phone. He should've turned the damn thing off. Cary glanced at the readout on the rental car's screen. Jules. Who else would it be? Fuck.

"What?" he barked.

"Jesus, boss. Have a Xanax or ten. Just letting you know the room's all rented out and taken care of. I'm getting my equipment set up now. You should be good to go in a day or two."

"Can you tell me how the fuck to get out of here while you're at it?"

He was met with silence. Cary wasn't surprised. He didn't do yelling. Not at Jules, not at anyone. He did charm. Charisma. Confidence enough to sell the hardest mark whatever lies and half-truths he happened to be peddling. Pissiness wasn't on Cary Talbot's résumé. He pulled over and took a deep breath. Then he took great pleasure in yanking his damn GPS cord out of the dash. He hated that thing.

"Powering off in ten seconds," the voice intoned.

Cary wanted to growl. Instead he took another long, slow, calming *goddammit* breath. "Sorry, J. Long day. I hate California," he grumbled.

"It's okay, boss. You hate everything. How on earth are you lost? The town is right off of highway twelve."

"I have no idea. I think this damn machine decided I was in Australia or something. Can you please just run a search on my tracker and tell me where the hell I am and how to get out?"

"Good thing we're paranoid." Jules laughed softly. "Give me a few minutes to get up and running, and I'll be able to tell exactly where you are. Get out of the car and do a sun salutation or something. You need to chill before you have a stroke."

Cary chuckled. "I'm not doing yoga on the side of the road under a bunch of goddamn grape leaves."

Jules made a derisive noise but didn't reply. Cary did prop the door of his rental car open, but all that got him was an overwhelming wave of dusty, late-summer heat that nearly made him choke. He took a long drink from his water bottle and chucked a few pistachios into his mouth. Chewing helped him calm down when he let himself get way too wound up. Some days he wished he'd never quit smoking.

"Where are we at with those directions, Jules?"

"Just... a... minute. There you are. Okay. So I'm going to need you to make a left."

"Jesus Christ, there is no fucking left."

Cary could tell Jules was holding back a laugh. "Okay, okay. Why don't we turn around? I'm going to try another way to get you back to highway twelve. I don't want you to end up crashed into the bottom of some wine vat."

Cary rolled his eyes and stuck his key into the ignition. "I don't even like wine but that's sounding better and better by the minute."

"I have no idea how you managed before you met me."

"Managed what?"

Jules's laugh came loud and clear through the car's speaker. "Anything."

By the time Cary reached their hotel—modest, nondescript and right off of the highway—he was hot and tired and beyond ready to have a big drink of anything strong, and pass out. That probably wasn't going to be his luck. Jules usually had about seven million details to work out with him when he least felt like talking. Plus he was hungry, and he wouldn't say no to some snacks.

Cary started to mentally prepare himself. He had a lot of work ahead of him, hopefully easy work, but work all the same. If he managed to pull it off, the payoff would be fantastic.

"What room are we in?" he asked Jules quietly. "Eleven fifteen. I'll prop the door open for you with the bolt." "Thanks. I'm on my way up."

Cary bypassed the front desk. He wasn't in the mood to put on a show, to charm the hotel staff into liking him but forgetting him the minute he was gone. He'd rather be completely invisible. Luckily he didn't need a card to make the elevator rise to his floor. There were ways around that. He knew ways around pretty much everything, but after the day he'd had, he really didn't feel like fucking around with gadgets.

True to form, Jules looked like she was about to stage a military coup right from the comfort of their hotel suite. Cary bitched and teased her about all her techy crap, but he didn't know how the hell he'd operated without her for as long as he had. She'd set up her computers and her phone station in the corner of the room, and had gotten comfortable in a pair of sweats, flip-flops, and a T-shirt. She'd tied her riot of inky black curls into a knot on the top of her head and was busily painting her toenails a bright pink. She glanced up when the door clicked shut.

"Hey, boss. You look like hell." Tactful as usual. Jules was brilliant at what she did, but smooth-talking was never going to be her strong suit. Good thing they had him for that.

"Thanks a million, Delgadillo. How are we looking?"

Jules chuckled at him. Typical. "I just got the system all set up. Give me a minute to breathe. You need a drink."

"And a nap. I think I have sun poisoning."

She smirked. "Hopefully it'll be raining when we get home."

Cary thought of his big, drafty loft in Portland, and smiled. He wasn't sure if you could call a place home if you were gone more than you were there, but there was something about the old building's weathered bricks, soaring metal-beamed ceilings, and scarred wood floors that felt like a refuge.

Jules went to the counter and opened a new bottle of scotch and pulled a fresh liter of soda out of the mini-fridge. She mixed Cary a drink without comment and handed it to him. He took a swallow and sank down onto the room's armchair gratefully.

"Thank you so much. This is literally going to save my life."

"That's why you pay me the big bucks." Jules rolled her eyes a little and gave Cary a fond smile. "You know. Bring you drinks and stuff. Answer the phone."

It was a running joke between them. That had nothing to do with why Cary had hired her. Jules was special. She'd been a sophomore at OSU and had a very promising future at some prestigious grad schools when she'd been caught doing a few very naughty things with her computer in the dorms. Like looking-for-backdoors-into-the-NSA's-internal-system kind of naughty. Cary would've thought that was impossible to do from a remote location. Apparently Jules had found a way to make it possible enough that some friendly government agents paid a visit to her dorm room the next day. Luckily she'd been out and saw them from down the hall. Jules had taken off, and Cary found her shivering and scared in a coffee shop, no family, no more scholarship, and newly homeless. He'd offered her a job, and she'd been with him ever since. She was like a kid sister, if by kid sister he meant an outrageous brat with an IQ of 180, limited social skills, and technology chops that made his head spin.

"So are we going to talk about the job?"

Cary sighed. "Now? Does it have to be now?" What was that he'd been thinking about her being a brat?

"Now would be good. Unless you'd like a nice stay off highway twelve for nothing. We need to get this job set up or we're wasting our time."

"Someday you're gonna kill me."

Jules snorted. No respect.

"So the plan is twofold, correct? Well, three actually. Get the mark to believe you work for the insurance company, but you're a little dirty. Introduce the idea that the Nine Sisters is just a myth. Falsify the tests to prove they're fakes. Oh, and then of course get them to sell the bottles to you at a low price to get them off their hands so they don't get charged with insurance fraud."

"That sounds about right."

It was a complicated game, and it relied on Jules's technical skills as much as his talking, but Cary thought they might be able to pull it off. He could barely fathom the payoff if they were successful. The Nine Sisters. Even one would be an incredible get. Nine of the world's most sought-after bottles of wine all in the same collection? Nearly priceless. Marigold Shelley was supposed to have them. Cary was banking on the fact that the rumors and Jules's techno sleuthing were, in fact, correct.

The story of the Nine Sisters was legend. It started back when George Washington had first taken office. He'd been a well-known fan of Portuguese Madeira wines. So much so that Pedro and Maria, king and queen of Portugal, had sent him a case of ten bottles of their private reserve Madeira. One had disappeared into time. Maybe it had been drunk by Washington himself, maybe broken or sold—that part of the story was never told. But the others had formed a collection. Priceless. Famed. Nearly mythical.

The bottles still had their royal seal from the Portuguese court on them, and the stamp showing they'd belonged to Washington's private collection. How a single vineyard owner got their hands on all nine of them was beyond Cary's imagination. Their worth was staggering. He had his work cut out for him if he wanted them to be his.

"I still don't like this, boss." Jules had never been one to hold back her opinion. She'd been making her opinion on the sisters known ever since Cary decided to go for it. "It's not fair."

"Jules. Marigold Shelley is reported to have one of the best private collections in the entire country. The Nine Sisters is the crown of that collection, but she has others. You know how I operate."

Cary might have been a con artist, but he had morals. He never took from people who couldn't afford to lose, and he never took everything. Not even close.

"But you're using the fact that she's distracted by her grandson to get to her."

"Of course I am. It's the perfect time. She's in love with the romance of getting her family back. She's not going to want to take time out of whatever years she has left to deal with me."

"And the kid? Hasn't he gone through enough after all these years?"

Cary shrugged. "He's twenty-four. That's not a kid. Plus, this isn't gonna hurt him. He doesn't even have to get involved."

He knew Jules had her reasons for wanting to protect Isaac, and they had a lot to do with her past. Cary didn't feel like playing cheap hotel room shrink.

"I've made you a cheat sheet." Jules handed it to him reluctantly. "I still don't like this, though."

"No kidding." She'd made her stance on the newest mark quite clear before she'd left Oregon a day and a half before Cary. "Do you want to go back to Portland and leave this to me?"

"No. You'll get arrested, and then what would I do? I'd be bored."

Cary sighed. "Contrary to your very strong beliefs, I did survive for thirty years before I found you at that coffee shop. Successfully."

Jules rolled her eyes. "How you managed that is a mystery I'm still trying to solve."

HE WOKE with the sun, like he had for nearly three months. His head spun every time he thought of where he was and what he was doing.

You've got this... Isaac. Your name is Isaac now.

Isaac. Every day he still had to remind himself of that. He was Isaac Shelley. Heir. Grandson of Marigold Shelley. Screwed to hell if he was ever made. So yes. Isaac Shelley.

Isaac got out of the huge bed in his room. He still couldn't believe it was his bedroom, his house, his life for a while longer. Hopefully, at least. Nothing had been signed yet.

He looked out the window at acres and acres of vines and hills and beautiful sun-kissed earth, and stretched, letting the warmth hit his skin. It was probably going to be another hot day. Only a few weeks until the harvest, according to the prickly vineyard manager, Kitty, whom he'd been trying to win over. He wondered if he'd still be around to see it or if he'd be long gone by then.

He showered quickly, dragged on a pair of perfectly tailored jeans, a polo, and casual but expensive shoes courtesy of Marigold, and left the house for his customary walk before the family and house staff met for breakfast.

Falling River Winery—the land, the house that had been nicknamed Torremolinos, and the outbuildings—had been in Sonoma since the thirties. Way before his time, obviously. Even before his newly inherited step-grandma's time. Isaac's research told him she'd married into the family when Isaac's father was a baby. The first Mrs. Howard Shelley had died giving birth to Isaac's father, and Isaac's mother never had a family that she knew. Sad, but convenient for him. No biological relatives meant no DNA testing. Made what could've been a nearly impossible job much easier, relying on his skill instead of science. *Isaac had been working at a little cafe on the main drag of Sonoma for a couple of weeks. It had taken some careful research and arranging a convenient job opening—he felt a little bad about making sure the last waiter lost his job so he could charm his way in, but he'd needed to be in the right place at the right time. Having Marigold find him was key. It would ring alarm bells if he went searching for her. He'd been polite to the customers in his short stay at the cafe, and good at his job, made sure the owner wouldn't feel hesitant to hand him one of their best patrons. After that, it was just a waiting game.*

The afternoon Marigold finally showed up had been slow. Isaac was about ready to pack it in when she walked in the door with another woman. They were seated in his section, which he wished he could take credit for, but really it was just luck working to his benefit. It only took one look at his face and she looked about to faint.

"Isaac?" Marigold whispered. Her face was ashen, her eyes wide like she'd seen a ghost. Isaac had to hold his grin inside. Looked like he was barely going to have to work at all.

"H-hi," he stuttered out. "Do I know you?" He was proud of how taken aback he could make himself look.

"You probably don't remember me, but I know you. You're my grandson." Marigold reached up to touch his face. The poor woman still looked like she was about to keel over. Isaac almost felt bad. Then he remembered he needed that trust fund and Marigold wasn't ever going to touch it.

"I don't have any family. Are you sure?"

"I'm positive. I'd know you anywhere."

He tilted his face up into the early morning sun. He was still pale, he always would be, but he'd gotten a dusting of freckles across his nose since he'd been working in the vineyard with the head farmer, Mike. The thought of one family owning so much helped him when he realized how much he liked Marigold and felt guilty lifting little Isaac's trust fund from her. She'd never miss that money. She hadn't looked at it in years. Isaac, on the other hand, had many uses for it. It was great how things worked that way.

After his walk, Isaac wandered into the kitchen off the main house. Gretchen, the cook, was putting out breakfast. It was usually delicious: eggs and some sort of toast, fruit, bacon or sausage, maybe even pancakes or crepes. Gretchen fed most of the main vineyard staff: Kitty, the manager; her assistant, Jose; Mike, the farm manager; and Tilly, who ran the equipment. Marigold sat at the head of the huge oak kitchen table like the benevolent matriarch that she was. Isaac still didn't feel like he belonged, after weeks of breakfasts with them, lunches, dinners, nights sitting with Marigold, the two of them just talking for hours. He still felt like he should hover.

"Isaac, darling. Come in. Gretchen made your favorite blueberry waffles."

Isaac smiled and walked toward the chair Marigold patted. There wasn't any hesitation in her smile. None at all. The employees greeted him with varying degrees of welcome. Gretchen, who'd been at the farm when the real Isaac was a boy, seemed just as eager as Marigold to bring him into the fold. Mike seemed to like him, and Tilly was indifferent as long as he stayed away from her machinery in the rooms where they pressed and stored the wines. Kitty, the manager? Well, that was different.

"Morning, everyone," Isaac said quietly. He slipped into his seat and reached for the jug of apple juice. He helped himself to a waffle from the plate Gretchen pushed across the table, as well as eggs and a few turkey sausages. He planned to follow Mike around the vineyard again. With his quick brain and the way Roman had trained him to learn details, he'd thought it would be easier to pick up the things he needed to know about the grapes and the wines they produced, but it hadn't been. At least the job didn't require him to know anything. Looking like a bumbling moron when it came to wine was probably best. It wasn't as if he needed to know anything about it long term.

"Hey, kiddo. Ready to learn some more about grapes?" Mike was big and burly, with graying hair, kind, pale blue eyes, and a thing for fancy beers. Even though Mike was years younger, something about him reminded Isaac of Roman. He'd liked Mike immediately. He was actually excited for another day on the vineyard with Mike. It felt… right, somehow. Like he was doing something real with his life rather than talking people out of their money.

Stop it. Isaac had been victim to about five million bouts of conscience since he'd gotten to Falling River.

"Of course. You coming along today, Marigold?" She gave him a look. "Sorry, Grandmother." It was hard to get used to calling her that, but she'd insisted.

"No, darling. I've made plans with a friend in town. Coffee and some shopping. I thought I'd take you to that gallery later this afternoon, though."

They'd been talking about a local gallery for a few weeks. Isaac loved art. His few memories of the dark times on the streets often had to do with hours and hours of staring into brightly lit art galleries, in awe of the colors and textures.

"I'd love that." Isaac shared a smile with Marigold. He couldn't believe how quickly she'd made him part of her life. It had taken one phone call and one astoundingly short cup of coffee before she'd started talking about him moving into the estate and calling Falling River his home. It had made his head spin. Of course, not everyone had been as trusting as Marigold, and no papers had been signed, but still. She treated him like he was one of her own.

Isaac finished his breakfast quickly when he saw Mike looking at him expectantly.

"Are you done?" Mike asked, which was his way of saying "if you're not done, grab a paper towel and put whatever you can carry on it because we're leaving."

"Yeah. I'm done. Thanks, Gretchen. That was delicious."

Gretchen nodded gruffly and grumbled about him being too skinny, like she had since the day he'd walked in the front door. Isaac smiled at the ground. With some of them, it was almost like he didn't have to work at all. They just… assumed he was for real.

"Please stay out of my office, Mike," Kitty said. "If you need anything, text or call." She smoothed her dark hair into a bun and smiled at Mike. Isaac didn't like her smile. It was a little cold. Mike didn't seem to have his problem with it.

"Sure thing, sweetheart. I don't want to ruffle all your papers."

Kitty smiled again. Isaac got the distinct impression she didn't like Mike any more than she liked him. She was his main problem. If she talked to Marigold and convinced her Isaac wasn't who he said he was, he was out on his ass. And Marigold trusted Kitty. He'd seen that already. He had to get to her. That was the answer.

"See you this afternoon, darling." Marigold waved as they walked out the door.

"You know," Mike said as he and Isaac were on the way to the truck he used to get along the vineyard's dusty roads, "I haven't said it, but I'm grateful for the fact that Marigold's found you. She lights up every time you walk into the room. I never saw her face look like that, and I've been here for over ten years."

"I'm glad I found her too," Isaac said. He felt a little twinge of guilt but pushed it aside.

It wasn't his problem.

CHAPTER 2

CARY HADN'T been to the wine country before. He'd never really seen a reason. Sure, there were rich people waiting to hand over their cash in the land of rolling hills and acres of grapes, just like everywhere else in the world, but it was such a pain. All the driving and the sun and dusty, meandering roads. Cary was a city guy. He liked noise and buildings, public transportation, trees in nice, neat little areas where they belonged. He liked the excitement of a new opportunity around every corner, not another long road to who the hell knew where. If he hadn't had his heart set on the Nine Sisters, he'd have found an excuse to leave the moment he got there. Probably even before Jules had to rescue him from being terminally lost in the middle of the grape vines. But Cary wasn't one for giving up. Especially not when he'd already used time and money to get there. He planned to see this damn thing through.

He saw the turnoff for the long drive into the Falling River Winery and took a deep breath. This was it. He'd spent the last two days going over details with Jules in their hotel room, and weeks before that prepping details for his character. He'd played the insurance auditor before—it wasn't a new role—but he never wanted to go in unprepared. He was going to be fine.

Cary thought he might have felt a twinge when he pulled onto the main drive for the vineyard. He told himself not to be ridiculous, but it felt different somehow. Maybe it was the promise of all that lovely money that waited for him if he was successful.

There was something about the place, he thought as he rolled past row after row of grape vines behind the white painted fencing. It wasn't any different than the other vineyards. Not really. All of them had rows of grapes and pretty gold grass and little dirt paths and roads winding through them. But the air seemed to smell different at Falling River, like sun and dust and green like everywhere else, but something sweet too, heavy and soft. Cary found himself liking it, and as much as he was annoyed by the hazy golden heat everywhere else, he rolled his window down and inhaled appreciatively. He liked Falling River. Maybe it was a good sign.

The house blended into the rolling hills somehow. It was Spanish style and stucco, painted a creamy yellow with thick beamed trim and decorated tiles around the windows and doors. That wasn't anything out of the ordinary for the location or the time it had been built, but again, there was something about the place that called him, made him want to put up his heels and relax with a book and a cup of coffee.

Cary shook himself. That wasn't him. It had never been him. He was energy and wanderlust; he was the guy with the home base he didn't call home, and more flight miles under more names than he could ever count. He didn't do coffee and books. He didn't do relaxation either. He needed to get his damn wine and get out before Falling River hypnotized him.

He hopped out of his rental, briefcase in hand, business cards in his pocket, ready to charm his way into Marigold Shelley's wine cellar. He took another long look around and inhaled one last time before he had to get in character. He was an auditor. He worked for an insurance agency. No problem.

I've got this.

Even though Cary the insurance auditor wasn't a huge stretch for him characterwise, he did his usual warm-ups, the typical method for sinking into the person he was meant to be. Cary the auditor was charming but methodical, gracious but exacting. He needed to get that across. It was almost as if he were an actor getting ready to walk onto the stage. But most actors couldn't get arrested if they flubbed a line. Small distinction.

The front door opened, and Cary was surprised it was Marigold Shelley herself. He would've expected it to be the housekeeper. The grande dame in places like this never answered her own door. Ever. He was pleasantly surprised. The lovely Mrs. Shelley looked just like she did in all the pictures online from the hundreds of charity events she seemed to attend each year. She was tall and willowy in an expensive flowing dress, still beautiful in her mideighties, pale white hair in a loose bun. She was exactly what Cary had expected. Except for the almost sweet expression on her face. Curious. Interested. Someone like her should look annoyed by his existence.

"Hi, ma'am. I'm Cary Talbot with Pembroke Insurance." Cary was an alias anyway. Nobody knew his real name other than the parents he hadn't seen in at least ten years. He'd always told them he sold insurance. Well... close enough. "We're performing a routine audit on the policy you have on your wine cellar. I'm assuming you received our scheduling call last week."

Marigold's forehead wrinkled in confusion. "I didn't actually. Isn't it a little early? You typically come in the late fall after harvest is over."

Cary was ready for that. They were early. He planned to be long gone by the time the actual agent showed up at the end of October. "Feel free to verify with my scheduler, ma'am." He handed her a business card with his name printed in neat navy blue typeface, an eight hundred number, and a four-digit extension.

"Let me go get my phone."

The number on the card connected to Pembroke Insurance. Usually. Of course Jules had rerouted that exact extension to their hotel room. Cary watched as Marigold walked to a phone on a console in the main hallway and dialed the number on the card. So far, so good. He knew he could work his magic if he just got a chance to get in the door. He heard Marigold talking.

"... No, I don't believe I got a message. I'm not very good at checking my voice mail."

He waited patiently while Marigold finished up with Jules. It was the perfect role for his assistant after all. Most call service workers were a bit impatient and not what you'd call charming. She fit the bill, to say the least. Marigold looked slightly annoyed but ready to continue when she hung up the phone. Cary had his foot in the door.

"I apologize for not being ready. Usually I'd have all our authentication documents ready to go."

Cary smiled, trying for gracious and patient, the opposite of Jules. Jules had pushed; he was open to pull Marigold in. "That's okay. I'm sure you know from the past, but it's a process to get all the wines authenticated again, check the paperwork, and reevaluate the policy."

Marigold shrugged delicately. "I'm not sure. My late husband handled these types of things."

Even better.

"Well, I'll try to get out of your hair as quickly as possible, but it might take me a few days to get through a collection of this size and value. We wouldn't want to make any mistakes." Cary tossed her an engaging smile. "Why don't we talk schedules. I could easily get started in the morning, if that works for you."

"Do you live in town?"

Cary smiled. "No, ma'am. I come from the regional offices up in Portland. I have a room for the week."

Marigold scoffed. "I have more guest rooms than I know what to do with. Why don't you stay here?"

Cary was speechless. Marigold Shelley was shaping up to be the easiest mark in the history of time. He figured he should protest for at least a moment or two. "I couldn't possibly. That's highly out of the ordinary."

"Nobody's ever accused me of being ordinary." Marigold winked at him.

"It'd feel like an imposition."

"Nonsense. I'll have Larissa put sheets on the bed in the guesthouse on the other side of the pool. That way you'll have your privacy. Of course you'll eat your meals with us. I have a marvelous cook."

He was flabbergasted. Cary hadn't run across many people at Marigold's social level who were as nice as she was. She may have been the first one, actually. "Are you sure about this? I am perfectly fine at the motel."

"Absolutely. Dinner is at seven. Why don't you go pack up and bring your things back here. We'll get you all settled before we eat."

Cary couldn't believe his luck. The more opportunity he had to be near Marigold, the easier his job would be. It was practically in his lap. It was perfect.

"Well, thank you. Really. I've never been invited to stay before. This is an honor."

She waved him off. "It's really no problem. Now go so you can make it back in time for dinner. I was thinking we might have it out by the pool tonight anyway. It's going to be such a lovely evening."

Cary simply inclined his head. "Thank you again. I'll be back in a few hours."

He waited until he was on the main road to dial Jules at the room. She picked up with her typical charming greeting.

"What's up, boss man?"

Cary had long since given up teaching her to do his job. It was probably best since he didn't have a clue how to do hers. Everything in its place and all that. "You're not going to believe this, Jules. Not even for a second."

"You decided to leave poor Marigold Shelley and her long lost grandson alone?" Jules said.

Cary didn't want another lecture about how these two weren't the right marks for them. How Isaac Shelley had been through too much already, how Marigold was almost too easy because she was distracted by her new family. How they seemed so much nicer than his typical marks. He didn't want to hear it. Not when this job was about to land right in his lap.

"More like I decided to accept when she offered me a room in the pool house while I conduct my audit."

Jules was silent for a few minutes. "You can't be serious. Nobody would do that."

"I know."

"That's, like, really odd. She doesn't even know you."

"I know."

"And you're not even a little suspicious?"

Cary shrugged, even though Jules couldn't see him. "No. I mean, I know the tells. I can see when someone thinks they're playing me. Either she's a master or else she's just a really unusually nice super-rich person."

"Maybe Marigold Shelley is the Black Mamba," Jules said slyly.

If he'd been drinking anything, he probably would've spit it out his nose. "Can you even imagine?" Carey asked, still chuckling. "I swear. Someday I'm going to make it onto that most wanted list and beat Black Mamba out of the top spot."

"Um, you know, sorry if I'm wrong and all, but isn't it best that the feds don't know you exist? You know, so you don't have them after you? Ever." Her voice dripped with irony.

"A little danger makes everything more exciting." Although Jules was right, he'd rather stay off the lists, thanks. All of them.

She made a distinctly unfeminine noise into the phone. It wasn't attractive. "I think I had all the excitement I can handle back in college."

It had taken Jules weeks to tell him the whole story—what she was capable of, what would probably happen if various government agencies found her. She'd checked her e-mails from a spoofed IP address a month or so after the dorm incident. Whatever she'd read was enough to make her close that account on the spot.

"C'mon," Cary teased, "That was four years ago."

"Still. Watch yourself at this place. Don't trust anyone."

"When have I ever trusted anyone but you? I don't plan to start. Anyway, it's a winery, not some secret government building."

"You don't know that."

"I'll be there in a little bit, okay? I'm starving. Have you ordered lunch?"

"Is that your way of saying you want pizza?"

"How about salad? I don't want to look rude, and dinner is in a few hours."

Jules snorted. "Salad and pizza?"

"Okay." Cary hadn't ever been able to say no to Jules. Or pizza.

ISAAC WASN'T aware of the fact that there'd been someone else in the house. He'd lain down for a short nap, as usual, after working with Mike and an afternoon with Marigold checking the reports the vineyard's accountant had prepared for them. Marigold had apologized and told Isaac it was a boring but regrettably necessary part of their lives, and she never let a month go by without being involved in her business and how it was being run. Isaac knew that was true. He'd seen her around the vineyard a lot, talking with Mike, with the laborers, chatting with Kitty, who was still giving him the glacial freeze after nearly two months.

Anyway, short nap, and the next thing Isaac knew, there was a nondescript rental car in the drive and a very, very noticeable man in the guesthouse on the other side of the pool. Isaac saw him when he glanced out the kitchen door. He'd just come out of the guesthouse and stretched into the sun. He was older than Isaac, probably about thirty. Could've been a little older or younger than that. It wasn't always easy to tell. Isaac couldn't see his face perfectly, but his sandy hair shone in the late-afternoon glow, and his body was beautiful, long and lean and broad shouldered in simple khakis and a button-down Isaac would really have liked to take off. The damn thing was ruining his view of what was sure to be an amazing torso.

"Enjoying the view?"

Marigold needed to quit walking so quietly.

"Um." Isaac blushed.

"He's a beautiful man," she said and elbowed Isaac. "I don't blame you."

Isaac blushed even harder. "I should probably grab a shower before dinner," he said instead of answering. He escaped to his bathroom before he could manage to let the newcomer know he was staring.

ISAAC COULDN'T take his eyes off the guy. He tried. Really. It wasn't like checking out the insurance auditor or whatever the hell he was could be any good for his job. His *job* was getting Marigold to trust him, not drooling over some guy that had to be bad news. And probably straight. But he'd always had a thing for blonds. And older guys. And anyone who could charm the hell out of a room and look like they were barely trying. Cary had it all in spades. He was hot, smart, charming, and in the middle of making Isaac's insides do dances he didn't know they could do. Dances he'd rather they didn't do. At least until his work at the vineyard was done and the trust fund was in his hand. Isaac had been trying to hang on to the most basic semblance of his role as the heir apparent ever since Cary had sat down across from him at the dinner table twenty minutes ago.

"Isaac?"

He realized Marigold was looking at him. Crap. She'd probably asked him some question and was waiting for an answer. Another great victory on the doing-your-job front. "I'm sorry. I spaced out for a minute. What did you say, Marigold?"

"I wish you'd call me Grandmother," she said.

"I feel a little weird doing it until we're sure." Isaac tried to look modest. Calm. Inside he was screaming *Yes! Yes! Yes! Call me your grandson, sign over the trust fund, let me get out of here.* Right? That's what he wanted, right? He'd decided the day Roman left and dropped this con in his lap that he'd go for the trust fund. Get the money, get out. There was no point in staying around playing house with Marigold after she got him what he needed.

Roman's "do what you want with the info" message had been a little weird. Sure, the long con of anyone's dreams would probably be to become part of a wealthy family. It was just the word "family" that screwed with Isaac's head. He'd tried that once with Roman and look how it worked out. He'd probably tried it when he was a kid too. He barely had any memories of that time other than flashes of dark hair like his and a big booming laugh that woke him up sometimes at night.

So no. No to taking on a new family. Yes to the trust fund. If he could stop acting like a love-struck teenager staring at his crush.

"I am sure. I have been since the moment I saw you. It just has to go through the proper channels before it can be official."

"What?" That was the first Isaac had heard of her doing anything legal about making him her grandson. Last he knew she believed it was him but that was about it. He was pretty damn sure the family lawyer, Kitty, and half the other people who had the right to an opinion thought he was the biggest fraud in the world. He wouldn't blame them. They'd be right.

"I figured I wouldn't tell you until I had it taken care of, but I'm working on it. That's probably all that matters right now."

"Oh. Wow." Isaac was a little surprised. He figured he'd have to work harder. It was almost... disconcerting. It wasn't over yet, though. "Anyway, what were you going to ask me?"

"Cary was telling me he'd need most of this week to catalog the wines in the cellar before he gets to work authenticating the bottles that have been added since the last agent's visit. I thought maybe you could help him." Marigold gave Isaac a sly smile.

Damn fucking hell. Was he really that obvious? Yeah, he'd been staring earlier but a little appreciation wouldn't be enough to have Marigold trying to play hook up. He had to be acting like he felt inside. Like a little boy with a huge crush. Isaac had thought he was better at the game. He hadn't been playing it all that long, but Roman had taught him better than to make cow eyes at some guy just because he was the prettiest man Isaac had seen in a long, long time. Damn.

"Um, *do* you need help?" He turned his best innocent but sad and emotionally bruised Isaac Shelley eyes at Cary. Might as well play into Marigold's good graces. She must've liked the idea of setting him up with someone.

Cary grinned at him. "Sure. I could use the company if nothing else."

There was something about his smile. Something compelling but weirdly familiar, almost like Isaac had seen it before.

"What exactly are you doing?"

"What your grandmother said. I'm going through the collection, checking it against our existing catalog, and working with the new bottles or ones that raise any red flags. We have several methods of checking provenance and authenticating them.

Mostly, you'd just help me keep my place in the catalog and maybe bring me a few bottles here and there."

Isaac doubted Cary needed any help at all. Still. "I can do that. I don't have any plans. At least not for a couple of days, right?" He knew there were a few events Marigold had wanted to show him off at. It was annoying, but she looked so happy to have him by her side, Isaac hated to bitch about what had really been a very easy job so far.

Marigold nodded and smiled slyly at him. Jesus.

"That sounds fantastic," Cary said. He gave Isaac another one of his blinding grins and speared an asparagus. "I'm guessing you'll be a lot of help. I bet you know a lot about the wines anyway. I just know the basics. None of the fascinating history."

Isaac felt his face heat. "Well, actually, I don't know that much. Marigold—"

"Grandmother."

"Um, sorry. Grandmother is teaching me more about the history of the vineyard and all of that, but I haven't been here very long."

"Still, I wouldn't complain if you joined me. It'll be a long couple of days down in the cellar if I'm all alone." Another smile, no less belly flipping than the rest.

What a flirt. Isaac had to admit he liked it. "Okay, I'll help you."

Isaac could've sworn he felt Kitty's glare. He didn't turn around to look. *Yeah, you don't trust me. I get the freaking picture.* At least if there was one person she was more wary of than him, it would be Cary. Kitty had given him the deep frost since the moment he walked through the door. Isaac kind of got it—well, with what he knew about Kitty and how she treated strangers. Cary was gorgeous, he was charming, and he had the kind of easy affability that seemed like the exact sort of thing that threw Marigold's estate manager into a distrustful hissy fit. Isaac wished Kitty would take a hike. She made his life about a million times harder just by existing, with her unpleasant, mistrusting stare.

"Darling, why don't you take Cary on a walk around the grounds after dinner? Show him the specimens Mike's been having you work on in the back garden. It'll be beautiful this time of night."

Isaac didn't have to know Marigold Shelley to know what she was doing. She wasn't even being subtle about it. Isaac hadn't seen such a hard sell since the last time he'd watch fences haggle over the price of a stolen painting. Still, had to give the woman credit. He'd shyly confessed to her a few weeks before that he didn't date women. Marigold had taken it in stride with a smile and a hug. Apparently she'd decided that while gay was more than okay, single was not.

"Grandmother. I'm sure Mr. Talbot has work to do to get ready for tomorrow. Papers or something."

"Not at all. I'd love a walk around the grounds. Falling River is gorgeous."

"The house is called Torremolinos, built to look like one of the original owner's favorite spots in Spain. Falling River is the winery. The main building is down the road nearly half a mile." Kitty managed to look judgmental, condescending, and irritated by Cary's lack of knowledge all at the same time. Isaac really, really didn't like her.

"Kitty," Marigold admonished. Isaac noticed she was gentle with her, more like a naughty child than an employee who'd been a huge pain in the ass to the insurance guy who could potentially make their lives a lot more difficult.

Kitty nodded in Cary's direction. "You'll enjoy the grounds, Mr. Talbot. They're lovely this time of year."

The concession looked like it had been dragged out of her by a whole herd of Marigold's prize Arabians.

Soon, dinner was over, and Isaac found himself out on the house's grounds with Cary Talbot, who somehow seemed like he'd be a bigger wrench in Isaac's plans than even cantankerous Kitty. There was something about him. Something that said danger. Well, danger in the best and worst possible ways.

It was quiet, and the sky was that purple-pink dusky color that came with the last of the light as the heat of the day faded into night, and it stretched for what seemed like forever. Isaac still hadn't gotten used to it. Everything he could see belonged to Marigold. Hills filled with neat row after row of vines that produced some of the best wines of the region. Someday he'd get used to it and quit being overwhelmed every time he looked out a window. Probably about the time when he had to leave. Most of Isaac hoped that was soon, before he was drawn in any further. But some hidden part of him wanted to stay forever. No matter how bad of an idea that was.

He felt like he should talk. Isaac had been working on his charm, but there was still a lot of the grubby street kid in him. Social situations weren't easy. It was part of why he was so perfect for the role of the missing Isaac Shelley. He didn't have to be charming, he just had to be... well, him. The kid who grew up on the streets and had no idea where he was from. Once or twice he'd even entertained the idea that maybe he *was* Isaac Shelley. Hell, he looked enough like the boy who'd disappeared all those years ago. But no part of the winery, of the house, or anyone in it was familiar. Surely, if he'd spent his childhood in and out of Falling River, some of it would have looked familiar.

"Did I hear you're just getting to know the place again?" Cary asked.

"Yeah." Isaac didn't know how much to tell, but he figured his story had been all over the papers. One more person couldn't hurt. "I actually don't remember it at all. I disappeared when I was a kid. I don't remember a lot of my childhood before I was about thirteen, just flashes and pieces. But I was working in a restaurant this spring, and Marigold came in. She recognized me in a heartbeat. I still have no idea if I really am her grandson. I've been to see a few doctors since I've been here, but it's not helping. I'm starting to think this is just the way it'll be from now on."

"But your name is Isaac?"

He nodded. "I had a name tag in my pocket with that name on it when I was a kid on the streets. Since they were the clothes I'd always had, I assumed Isaac was me."

That was a lie. So was the part about the restaurant. He had been there, but it wasn't exactly an accident he'd picked the restaurant Marigold frequented with her friends to find a job. He'd been found on purpose, a very well-constructed accident. And he'd become Isaac. It had all been surprisingly easy, which made him a little nervous to be honest. According to Roman, the easy jobs always ended with the biggest wrenches in the works.

"Must be intimidating to walk into all of this," Cary said, gesturing to the gardens and the vineyard.

"It was. Still is, even after all these weeks. But I really like Marigold. Even if I don't remember her, she's kind of what I imagined my family would be like… well, other than the money. I didn't imagine that."

The weird part was, it was true. Isaac had always imagined a grandmother a lot like Marigold. And parents too, loving and a bit frazzled, rushing out the door with kisses and his lunch and reminders to turn in his math homework. He'd spent long nights in San Francisco when he was a kid wondering if all of that was just wishful thinking, or if those people really were out there somewhere for him and he just couldn't quite remember them.

"I bet it's been great to find her."

Isaac tried to school his face into a shy smile. Honestly, he did feel a little awkward about talking to someone about Marigold. He figured he'd never be as good as Roman. "Yeah, it's great. I wish I'd known her all along. She's been so nice to me since I got here."

Isaac inhaled. He was used to the baked, dusty smell of summer and the grapes that seemed to permeate the air, but there was something new, warm and soft, a little citrusy, very appealing. It had to be Cary. Isaac leaned a little closer. "Do you want to see the roses? It's a little dark, but it'll still be nice out there. Marigold has been working on them for years, I guess."

"Sure. I can take a look."

Isaac tried not to stumble like a moron as he led Cary down the stairs to Marigold's prize roses.

AFTER A pleasant but somewhat quiet walk through the gardens, Cary left the shy and very pretty Isaac at the door to the main house and ambled across the yard and around the huge tiled pool to his beautiful little guesthouse. He slid the doors shut and made sure nobody was listening before he pulled his phone out of his pocket and dialed his partner. He flopped down on the huge cushy bed and waited for her to answer.

"Hey. What's up?" she finally said when he thought maybe she'd gone to bed. He'd been just about to hang up when he heard her voice.

"Jules, this is going to be a piece of cake. Like cake with squishy cream cheese frosting." He grinned up at the high beamed stucco ceiling and tried not to get ahead of himself.

"Good. I'm already tired of this town. It fucking creeps me out. Everything is so perfect. I don't know what to do with perfect."

"Yes. Because Portland is so scarred and gritty."

Jules made a noise in the back of her throat. "You know what I mean. It's like Touristville here."

"Well, then let's get to work. I'm in. I'm so in. I'm supposed to start cataloging the collection tomorrow. This job is in the bag."

"And the plan is we plant the chatter online so it's ready to find. It'll just take some well-placed articles and blog comments to get them believing the sisters might not be real over the next few days."

"Yep. Like I said. No problem. I have a feeling Marigold is a tough old cookie, but she has a weakness, and I think I can use it to our advantage."

"What's her weakness?" Cary heard wariness in Jules voice. She was right to be wary. She sure as hell wasn't going to like his solution.

"Easy. Isaac."

"Cary…."

"What? It's perfect. I think the kid's got the hots for me, and it's no hardship for me to get a little closer to him. Marigold even has set it up so he's going to help me catalog in the morning. He doesn't know much about the collection, he's already admitted it. I can sway him. If I get him on my side, it'll be that much easier to win her over. She's still so much in love with the idea that she has a grandson. It'll be a tipping point once he's on board."

"Cary…."

"You know what? You can keep saying my name, but I still think he's our best doorway in. I don't want to discuss it."

"But—"

"But nothing. I need you to work on the Internet stuff. We'll need stories of people who researched the sisters and came across collections that were supposed to be real. We need—"

"Jesus fucking Christ, Cary," Jules snapped. "You'd think I didn't know how to do my job. Charm the old lady, make out with the grandson, and let me get the real work done."

Cary knew when Jules was angry with him. She wasn't very good at hiding it. "Thanks, Jules," he muttered. Because, yes, she worked for him. To a point. But they both knew how much easier she made his job. He waited for her reply. It didn't come.

"Jules?"

Cary pulled his phone away and saw the home screen staring blankly at him. She'd hung up.

CHAPTER 3

ISAAC COULDN'T stop thinking about dinner the night before. Well, he couldn't stop thinking about Cary. Cary's blond hair, his glamorous smile, and the way he'd managed to look at Isaac a lot but still include Marigold and the frosty Kitty in his conversation. He wondered if Cary had noticed him the same way. Then he got really annoyed with himself for thinking about a guy when he had work to do. Again. Always.

Isaac yanked on a polo, one of the preppy, well-cut ones Marigold had picked out for him a few days into his stay. He'd had clothes—he and Roman had been doing very well—but Marigold assured him it was one of her ways of showing affection. She'd been missing the opportunity to mother him for ten years, and she wanted to buy him expensive outfits even if he already had everything he needed. Marigold hadn't wavered. Everything she did, everything she said, told him she thought he was really Isaac Shelley. That he was really her grandson. As far as Isaac was concerned, Marigold was taken care of. He had to deal with the other people in her life, the ones who'd convince her not to file the paperwork, or the ones who would maybe help the papers not pass through. That was a little harder. Complicated multimark cons had always been more Roman's game. Trial by fire, Isaac supposed. He pulled on trim trousers and a pair of expensive canvas sneakers, and spent more time trying to calm his dark hair than he usually did. It had nothing to do with Cary. Nothing at all.

"Morning, everyone," he said when he got down to breakfast. The usual spread was out: eggs and sausage, english muffins, fruit, juice and coffee.

Cary was already at the table, talking animatedly to Marigold, hands waving around. He looked up when Isaac walked in and smiled his big charming grin before he went back to Marigold.

"What are you doing today, sweetheart?" Marigold asked him.

"I thought I was going to help Cary catalog the wine bottles. Wasn't that the plan?" Isaac tried to sound casual about it. After all, Cary wasn't the actual reason he was here. It helped if he kept telling himself that instead of staring.

Cary smiled at him and raked his sandy blond hair off his face. "Like I said, I'd really appreciate the company," he replied. "I'll be doing some paperwork this morning, but I'll be down there all afternoon if that works for you."

"Sure," Isaac said. *Relax. You have one job to do. Time to do it.* Isaac chose to sit next to Marigold and pour her a refill of orange juice.

"Thank you, darling," she said. She patted Isaac on the knee.

"Of course." As usual he tried to ignore Kitty's death glares. She was constantly around, like he was going to do bodily harm to Marigold if she let her eyes sway for more than a little while. It was bullshit. Isaac wondered if Kitty's animosity was starting to work in his favor, though. Marigold had dismissed Kitty more than she'd listened lately. He must've been better at his job than he thought.

He didn't have much to do after breakfast. Mike had a lot of work to do in his office, Marigold was busy, and Kitty... well he'd like to stay away from her as much as he could, thanks. The best thing he could think of was to go out and enjoy the pool he'd only been in a few times. Isaac went to his room and stripped out of the clothes he'd chosen so carefully earlier. He put on a pair of swim trunks, a T-shirt, and some flip-flops, grabbed a towel and sunscreen, and hit the stairs at a jog.

"Going for a swim, dear?" Marigold asked. She had her laptop open in front of her and was typing away at the keys.

"Yeah, I figured I'd stay out of everyone's hair."

"That's nice, sweetheart. Don't forget sunscreen."

"I won't, Grandmother."

"I'm sure Cary will enjoy the show."

Jesus. "I can't believe you just said that."

Marigold looked up at him innocently. "What? I'm old, not dead."

"You don't even know that he likes men."

"Yeah. No clues at all." She snorted. "Go swimming, darling. I'll talk to you in a little bit."

It was bright out, as always. Isaac stripped down to his shorts and slathered his pale skin with sunscreen. He'd tan eventually but pink was his typical reaction to any type of sun. He knew he wouldn't last long on a deck lounger without at least a few minutes in the pool first, so he bit the bullet and jumped in.

The water was freezing at first, but then it felt great. He floated on his back and looked up at the huge blue sky. Isaac wasn't going to lie to himself. Sometimes he was tempted to stay in this huge house and pretend to be Marigold's grandson forever. He didn't really miss his loft or San Francisco. He missed Roman, but he wasn't waiting back in the city. But while it was nice to imagine being Isaac Shelley, vintner and heir, the fear that one day his jig would be up and he'd be back at square one was just a little too big for him to say fuck it and jump right in. It was definitely best to stick with the plan.

"WHAT ARE you doing with each of these again?"

They'd been in the wine cellar for about ten minutes. Mostly in that time, Cary had wandered around and just looked. He couldn't help it. Wine buff or not, the place was fantastic. It had been built around the arched foundations of the house above. The floor was smooth stone, the stones in the arches worn with time and covered in places with a thin layer of aging stucco. Somebody must've spent a fortune on the wine racks. They were custom-built and nestled against the walls between low-burning light fixtures. In the middle of the room was a big old banquet table, polished to a high shine and surrounded by low stools. It had taken him a few minutes to get over his awe, but get over it he did. He had to get to work. At least he had to look like he was.

Cary put the bottle down on the table. He wasn't doing much, honestly, but it had to look authentic. "I'm scanning each bottle's label and comparing it to the list and photographs we have on file. I'm not an appraiser, but I'm here to look for any discrepancies. If it's necessary, we will call an expert in to verify authenticity of a bottle. I've had to do it lots of times."

Isaac seemed to buy that explanation. Cary liked the idea of having Isaac with him more and more, despite Jules's misgivings. He didn't know enough to question Cary's methods further, and he'd lend a bit of authenticity. Also, he was really fun to look at. Cary had noticed Isaac staring at him, and he didn't object to looking back. The kid had a gorgeous smile, and his dark hair, pale skin, and huge sea blue eyes were hard to miss. Plus those lips. It was really hard not to stare at them. Cary wouldn't mind spending a while kissing Isaac and his pretty, soft, puffy lips. He was fairly sure Isaac wouldn't object to that either.

"Here, look at this." Cary handed Isaac a bottle of Château Lafite and made sure to drag his fingers lightly over the backs of Isaac's fingers as he pulled away.

Isaac shivered lightly. "It's chilly down here, isn't it?" he asked nervously.

Cary knew that wasn't it at all. He wasn't going to lie and say the touch didn't affect him too. He bit his lip. "The bottle you have is really gorgeous. Château Lafite from 1945."

"How much is it worth?" Isaac stroked the label and the glass like he was looking for hints of something special. Cary didn't know much about wines at all, other than what Jules had shoved down his throat during their mini crash course, but even he could tell there was something different about the bottles in Marigold's collection. They felt important.

"Two thousand is what we have on file, although I think they've appreciated a bit since this last audit."

Cary checked the paperwork Jules had been able to get for him. Marigold Shelley's inventory, and the appraised value of each bottle, had been itemized in neat numeric order according to its place in the cellar. It was almost like a library. Cary checked off the bottle on his list, did a few checks, and scanned the label.

"Jesus. Really?"

Cary nodded and watched Isaac, who felt the label and handed it back. "You know, I think wine is nice and all, but I don't really get it. I mean, it's just grape juice, isn't it?"

"It's a very special old bottle of grape juice." Cary winked at him.

"Are all these bottles worth this much?"

Cary chuckled. "No. Actually, they're not. We have a long way to go before we get to the top. The crowing jewel of the collection is worth... well, quite a bit more. Let's just put it that way. I can barely believe it exists. I've been hearing about it for years, but I thought the thing was a myth."

There, drop the first hint. Get him thinking about it even if it's at the back of his mind. Isaac's eyes grew wide. "What is it?"

Cary chuckled. "I thought you didn't know anything about wine. Even I know what your grandmother supposedly has, and I'm clueless when it comes to these."

"I can appreciate something if it's worth that much money. I don't need to be an expert."

"I didn't even tell you how much."

"You don't have to. Quite a bit more than two thousand for a bottle of alcohol is enough to impress me any day."

Cary reached for another bottle, one he knew a bit about from his research. "Look at this one. It was produced right here at Falling River during prohibition." He sighed appreciatively. He'd always had a healthy respect for the rule breakers. "They produced and sold them right under the government's nose. There was hardly anything here then, I bet. Just some grapes and a dusty shack in the middle of nowhere. It shouldn't be worth more than the glass it comes in, but it's a piece of history."

Isaac looked at the bottle, with its old hand-printed label and wavy glass. "So my great grandfather made this? If he even is my great grandfather, that is."

"Sure did. Great family story, isn't it? I wish my great grandpa had made hooch during prohibition." Cary turned his best smile on Isaac. Most people couldn't resist it. Isaac smiled shyly back. Either he was the most unassuming kid in the whole world, or he was really laying it on thicker than thick with the shy act.

"What did he do?"

"My great grandfather? Stocks I think. Nothing important. Or very interesting."

Isaac handed the bottle back. Cary brushed his thumb along Isaac's wrist to test the waters. Isaac smiled at him again and touched the spot with his own questioning hand. Cary was in. He handed him another.

"A bottle of Moët from the late 1800s. It has one of the original labels drawn by Mucha. Beautiful, isn't it? I wish they still used them." Cary handed Isaac yet another bottle. Isaac inspected it before he handed it back slowly. Their fingers brushed again, slow and shivery in the cool, temperature-regulated darkness of the wine cellar. They leaned closer, their breath lingering and blending over the old bottle. Isaac's lips fell open, soft and surprised. Cary wanted it. Isaac obviously wanted it too. *Kiss him. Do it now.*

DON'T KISS him, you moron. Don't do it....

Isaac hadn't ever wanted to kiss someone so badly in his entire twenty-four years. The need had been building since the first moment he'd seen Cary stretching by the pool, and it had only gotten stronger. Hotter. More intense.

To be fair, he'd spent a lot of his past trying to survive. Scrounging for food didn't exactly leave time for romance. And once Roman found him, he was busy learning everything he could. He'd bounced from mark to mark, never relaxing long enough to do anything but finish the job. Roman had been proud. Isaac had slowly been building up a pretty substantial store of cash. Things were going well. He didn't need Mister Suave Hot Insurance Guy to mess up what could potentially be the job to set him up for life.

"Are we done with this bottle?" he asked. Isaac was annoyed by how husky his voice sounded. Jesus. Maybe if he just said "throw me down on the wine cellar floor and take me now," it would be easier. He looked at his hands. Empty. Yes, he'd already given the bottle back to Cary. Even better.

"I'd say so." Cary's voice was husky too. He reached up and cupped Isaac's face. "Can I?"

Against his better judgment, and Roman's voice playing in his mind, Isaac nodded. He leaned forward and brushed his lips against Cary's. Cary threaded his hand into Isaac's hair and kissed him again, and then again, little sucking kisses that made Isaac's blood race and his body want more. He couldn't remember the last time he'd been kissed, but it sure as hell couldn't have been so delicious. Maybe it was the dark and the cool air. Something was going to his head.

Cary tugged lightly at his hair, and Isaac opened his mouth. He felt Cary pushing gently and walked backward until he bumped up against one of the sloping arches that framed the room. Cary plastered Isaac's body gently with his own and deepened the kiss. He rubbed Isaac's sides. Isaac heard a moan and realized it was his own. He held on to Cary's hips and simply let it happen. Kissing the insurance guy—no, the super-hot, charming older insurance guy was probably a horrible choice when it came to doing what he was there to do, but Isaac didn't care. He wanted to keep kissing forever.

Cary leaned into him, trapping him against the wall. He deepened the kiss further and further until they pulled apart, breathing hard.

"I probably shouldn't be doing this," Isaac murmured.

"I probably shouldn't either. I'm the one who would get fired over it."

"So… we're stopping?" he asked. He wished he didn't sound quite so pathetic. *Yes. You're stopping.*

Cary didn't answer. He simply pulled back and gave Isaac a rueful smile. Isaac nodded and tried to calm his raging pulse.

They went back to wine bottles after that, cataloging and taking pictures of labels to match up with his collection. It wasn't exciting. He couldn't believe Cary's whole job was doing this.

Wine, jewelry, old books, cars… it must get really tiring to spend every day doing the same thing over and over.

"I think that's probably enough for today. I got about a fifth of the way through."

"Does it always take this long?"

Cary shook his head. "Your grandma has a huge collection with a lot of rare bottles." He smiled then, one of those disarming smiles that said he was trustworthy and the kind of guy Isaac could hang out with no expectations. Isaac wanted to haul him back in for a million more kisses. Life wasn't fair.

CHAPTER 4

"HEY."

Isaac looked up from where he'd been about to hop off the bottom stair of the narrow back stairwell. His eyes were huge and blue and surprised. Cary didn't notice how long and curly his eyelashes were. Not at all.

Of course, they'd bumped into each other in what might have been the only narrow hallway in the entire house. The one that led up the back stairs behind the kitchen to the family rooms on the second floor. Good timing, that. Cary smiled to himself. Hopefully he hadn't been too obvious about it.

Isaac had been trotting down the stairs, hair damp, khaki shorts and another well-cut preppy shirt on, but crew neck this time instead of the polos he'd been in the past few days, feet shoved into fresh, bright white canvas shoes. He looked like everything he was supposed to be: a modern aristocratic young man with tons of money and a casual appreciation for nice things. Cary wanted to tear him out of each and every one of those nice things and lick him. Like every part of him. A lot. Inconvenient but maybe still useful as long as he kept control of himself. Cary still couldn't believe his crazy luck. He might have to thank the con job gods for getting him into such a perfect setup. After the job was done. No use getting cocky before the bottles were in his hand and Falling River in his rearview mirror.

"Hi," Isaac said quietly.

"Morning." Cary made his voice as rough and appealing as he could. He cupped Isaac's face, drew his fingers across smooth skin, and then dropped his hand like he'd just remembered he wasn't supposed to touch. That they weren't going to do this thing, whatever it was.

They were so going to do it.

Cary was going to enjoy every single second of it, too, but not too much, of course. Then he was going to make sure Isaac helped him convince Marigold he was telling the truth about her precious wines. Yes. They were definitely doing this thing. Isaac just needed a bit of convincing.

"How'd you sleep?" he asked.

"Not that well. Okay, I guess. I kinda...." Isaac blushed like a teenager, and Cary felt a tiny twinge of guilt.

It was too easy. Way too easy. Didn't mean that would stop him. Isaac wasn't the mark. He was just someone who would help him get to the mark. A bit of collateral damage. Not even that. They could both have a little fun and none would be the wiser at the end, right? Cary tried not to hear Jules's disapproval in his head. As much as they typically ended up doing exactly what he wanted, she still had the power to make him feel really bad about it if she didn't agree. Especially because she didn't disagree very often. Cary pushed his opinionated assistant out of his head as much as he could and tried to look concerned.

"Why didn't you sleep well?"

"I couldn't stop thinking about things. Like... yeah. Things." The poor guy couldn't spit out a whole sentence. Cary wondered what he'd been doing before his grandmother fished him out of whatever back channel he'd been swimming in. Didn't seem like dating was one of those things. The kid had zero game. It was kind of adorable.

"Things like kissing me? Because I spent all night thinking about kissing you. And thinking about how I wanted to do it again. I still want to kiss you again." He knew he was laying it on a little thick, but damn if it wasn't going to work. Cary couldn't pull out of this one without making a big mess. It had to work.

"Me too. I want to kiss you. It's just not a good idea. I'm new here, with my grandma and you're here and… you know. Work." Isaac looked so flustered. Cary cupped his face again. His skin was soft and warm and pretty, and he really liked touching it.

"I know. Bad idea. We've been over that. But…." He trailed off and leaned closer.

Isaac had this moment where "fuck it" flew across his expressive face in the most obvious way, and then he dove in for a kiss. A long, breathless kiss that knocked the kiss from the day before way out of the water. Cary shivered. So he didn't have much game, but Isaac Shelley sure as hell knew how to use his mouth to wreak havoc on Cary's entire body. Isaac wound his fingers into Cary's hair and pulled. Hard.

"Just so you know, this really, really is a bad idea," Isaac said one more time, breathless and wet-lipped.

"I know. I don't care."

He chuckled softly against Cary's mouth. "Me neither."

"So we keep kissing?" Cary asked. He rubbed his lips over Isaac's and nipped softly. Then he went back for another. Another. More kisses, more breathing. Just more.

He couldn't goddamn believe himself.

Yeah, seduction was part of his act a lot of the time, and he'd always been very good at it with men and women, but he was breaking the first fucking rule he'd ever learned, the first rule he'd teach any student. Just the first damn rule, period. Never ever fall for your own con. Never. And Cary was falling for these breathless kisses as much as Isaac was. At least mostly as much. He was feeling it. He was getting caught up in the racing hearts and the faint breath and the heat crawling up his spine from what amounted to some middle-school-level making out in the back hallway of Marigold's house but was somehow hotter than anything he'd ever done. Yeah, he was fucking feeling it. He hadn't felt more than "thanks for getting my rocks off" in years. This was nothing like that, and it had to stop.

Cary's head wasn't making sense. His motivations had clouded in the space of a few brushes of Isaac's lips. Isaac was right. It was a really, really bad idea. But he'd made it part of his plan, and he had to go forward with it. At least that was what he told himself.

Cary leaned into Isaac again and kissed him, more gently this time. Less teeth, less desperation. More seduction. He could keep control of this thing between them, use it to his advantage. Not get sucked in. He was a goddamn professional.

"I like kissing you," he said between slow sucks of lip and nipping teeth. He did like kissing Isaac, obviously. More than he should. Far more than he should. It was the truth. At least he was following one of his rules while he was breaking another. And that was to tell the truth. Yeah, ha-ha. The grifter telling the truth. Irony at its best. But really. As often as he could use the truth, he did. Made the lies easier to sell if there weren't too many of them.

"I like kissing you too," Isaac whispered. He played with the soft hair on the back of Cary's neck, like he already knew that was one of Cary's weak spots. Like he meant to pull him in closer with every little tug and tease. Fucking hell. "Why'd you stop?"

Cary wasn't sure he had a coherent answer for that question other than "you're sucking me in and you don't even mean to." "Because we're supposed to go to breakfast. With everyone else."

"Oh. Yeah." Isaac grinned. "Why were you back here?"

Because I was engineering a meeting with you of course. What do you think? "I'm not sure. I was looking for the bathroom."

"Right." Isaac didn't look like he bought that at all. His grin grew, if anything. It was annoyingly cute. "You forgot it's on the other side of the kitchen?"

"Uh. Yeah. I forgot."

"That's what I figured."

Isaac giggled into another kiss, pulled Cary's body closer and wound his arms around Cary's neck. Isaac had the size advantage in that moment; standing on the bottom step of the staircase gave him a few inches of height, but he still felt fragile somehow in Cary's arms, like someone Cary wanted to protect. Damn. No. Not even close to what Cary wanted to do. None of that shit.

He sank into the kiss and cradled Isaac closer, like it was their first kiss, like it was the thing he'd been thirsting for all night. He got lost in Isaac's taste, in his breath, and the way Isaac's skin felt when Cary slid his hands under his shirt.

"I can't believe I'm doing this," Isaac whispered. "It's like the teenage sneaking around I never got to try."

"If you can't believe it, guess how I feel," Cary said dryly.

Isaac giggled again. Cary hated how much that giggle got to him.

"I bet. What are you, twenty-seven?"

I'll take that. "Not quite, kid. But thanks for the compliment."

"Like I care how old you are. You're hot." Isaac kissed him again. And this time all his fragile softness somehow turned to clingy, sexy minx. Cary was thrown off. How did Isaac waver between unpracticed and expert? How did he keep Cary so off his damn game?

He drew Isaac in for another kiss, happy to do more research. They were just getting back into it when a surprised squeak had Cary jumping off of Isaac like he really was back in his teens, hiding his conquests from his parents.

"Oh. Oh."

Cary looked up. Marigold. Jesus. Not part of his plan. Marigold was not supposed to see her damn insurance auditor putting the moves on her twenty-four-year-old grandson. Now she wouldn't trust Isaac's judgment when it came to the wine if she knew he was in the middle of a sex haze free fall. He backed up and wiped his suddenly sweaty palms on his pants and tried to swallow around the lump in his throat. How could he let his hormones carry him away like that?

Isaac bit his kiss-plumped lower lip. "Morning, Mari— Grandmother, I mean." Despite his protestations the day before, it seemed like Marigold had won that battle.

She smirked. Her surprise had melted into a smug, knowing grin. "Morning, darling. I see at least two of us are having a good one."

"Oh God." Isaac put his face in his hands, and Cary stepped back again. He remembered a moment that had been singed into his memory for years. Seventeen, caught in his girlfriend's room by her parents in only his jeans. Shirt, socks, and shoes somewhere on the floor. He'd never quite lived that moment down in his mind, or the ones that came after that with her dad chasing him out of the house with a golf club. He wasn't thrilled to be reliving them. At least Marigold was amused rather than angry, and he and Isaac were full-grown adults. He wasn't sure if that made making out in the back hallway better or worse.

"Um. Let's go ahead and get some breakfast before we start on the wines again."

"Wines." Marigold snickered. "Wines."

At least she seemed like she was fine with their little romance. He just had to make sure she still trusted Isaac. Isaac, who looked like he was about to choke. "Grandmother. Come on, I'm hungry. I'll pour your juice."

Cary watched Isaac sling his arm over Marigold's shoulders and lead her into the kitchen where she couldn't see Cary's flaming face. Jesus. Not what he had planned.

Way to go on the smooth seduction, man. You nailed that one on the head.

IT WAS a very embarrassing breakfast. Isaac still wasn't sure he had gotten over it. He didn't know if he ever would. On one hand, Marigold had seen a part of him that was very real and didn't seem to mind. On the other, well, yeah. Embarrassing. Especially when she kept throwing them sly looks and asking Cary if he wanted another sausage. Seriously. Sausage. Isaac couldn't handle it if she didn't stop. Apparently the lack of adult supervision he'd had in his teens hadn't prepared him for teasing, even of the loving variety. He wanted to die.

He crept down the stairs to the wine cellar with Marigold's laughing eyes burning a hole in his back. He found Cary at the bottom, trying to hold back his own laughter.

"God, that was uncomfortable."

"I know." Isaac broke into a chuckle. He couldn't help laughing now that it was over. "If she'd made another sausage joke, I think I might have melted into the floor. Sausage. Jesus."

"I know. And the way she looked at me when I left the table to set up for the day. Like we were going to strip down and fuck the second you got down here."

Isaac blushed a little at that. It wasn't that he'd never been with anyone. He wasn't a baby. He had experience. At least some. But he hadn't been with a grown-up. Mostly just kids like himself, messing around and trying to figure shit out on their own. And then for a long time, there hadn't been anyone in his life other than Roman, who was a grandfather figure more than anything else. The thought of romance with someone nearly Marigold's age would've made him laugh. Or heave.

"Okay. Where were we?" Cary asked. Isaac blushed again. "With the wines. The wines."

Isaac giggled again, just like Marigold had.

"Yeah. The wines. I think we were on that shelf over there." He gestured to a shelf in the corner where he remembered them leaving off the night before. Honestly, all he could really remember was that damn kiss and how much he'd wanted more of them. The shelf didn't seem to matter much in retrospect. "Yeah. That's where we were."

"Hey, boss."

"Jules. What's up? You can't call me here unless there's an emergency. I don't know when I'm going to be around Marigold or Isaac." Cary had just gotten into his guest cottage after a long day of pretending to catalog wines. Actually, he was really doing it. Had to make the whole thing look good, right? And hours of photographing labels and checking them against inventory had made his back ache and his head smart. He was never using this cover again. It was a pain. Literally. He pounced onto the amazing bed and lay there staring at the ceiling.

Jules chuckled on the other side of the line. "Ooh, Isaac."

"Since when did you stop hating me for using poor, sweet Isaac."

"I'll let you know," she said with an audible smirk.

"Shut it. Seriously. And really it's not a good idea to call me here unless there's an emergency."

"Yeah. You've said that about a million times. I know."

More like twice, but he wasn't going to correct her. That was a lesson he'd learned early on. "Well?"

"What?"

"Why'd you call?" Cary swore sometimes she wasn't worth putting up with. Okay, he never really thought that. Cary was dead without her. He'd managed to last for a few years before he met her, but he knew he'd been on the precipice of being totally screwed for most jobs.

"Oh. Yeah. There's something shifty going on at Falling River. More specifically, at Marigold's house."

"Torremolinos?"

"What?"

"That's the house's name. Torremolinos."

"Tiramisu what? Whatever. Anyway yes. I've been looking around, trying to make sure everything is open for us, and I've found a few things. Being sold through the usual channels, all from her estate. Nothing big, traded for cash. Barely a whisper."

"Wait." Cary didn't like the sound of that at all. "You think someone's stealing from Marigold? Someone other than us?" That had the potential to screw things up majorly. Cary wasn't in the mood to deal with some amateur.

"Yes, boss. That's what I said. What are you doing over there? Drinking all the wine?"

Cary chuckled even though nothing about what Jules had told him was funny. "Shut up. Again. When did this start?"

"As far as I can tell, about a month ago. There were only a few things at first, scattered here and there, but it's picked up in the past week. Three things. Through Sandro. A tray, some earrings I believe, and a necklace."

Cary knew that name. "Sandro? Isn't he that fence down in San Fran? I thought he was quiet."

"He is quiet. We've used him before. He's one of the best."

"Then how did you know someone was going through him?"

Cary didn't have to be with Jules to see the face she always made in his mind, impatient eye roll and all. "Because I know."

"And you're sure it's items from Marigold's house?"

"I have her insurance lists. I'm sure. Claims have been made on at least four of the missing items. I'm not sure she's noticed the newest ones yet."

"You don't think it's Marigold, do you? Making claims on her own things?" Cary had looked at her financials. Marigold didn't need the money. She was doing far more than fine.

"No, dimwit." Another nearly audible eye roll. "I think it's Isaac."

Cary couldn't believe that hadn't been his first reaction. Isaac. Of course. The missing grandson comes in off the street and suddenly Marigold's private treasures are being sold through the quietest fence on the West Coast. That anyone with a bad background would… actually no. He wouldn't have access to him. Sandro worked with the pros, not with ratty kids off the street.

"How the hell do you think Isaac knows the best fences in the area? He was just a street kid."

"And you're just an insurance auditor. Cary, don't be dumb."

No fucking way. "He's not running a con. I know what a con looks like. That kid couldn't act his way out of a paper bag."

"Correction, boss. You know what a bad con looks like. There have to be ones out there who can fool you."

"If he's stealing jewelry from someone who would give him everything, he's not a con artist, he's a moron. Or else he's a really messed up kid who's never gotten over years of nearly starving." Cary felt a sharp pain in his gut.

"Just check him out, okay?"

Cary thought of that morning, of the kisses and the touches and how they'd spent nearly an hour plastered up against the wine cellar's walls kissing like they couldn't stand the thought of breathing their own air. Isaac. Shit. As much as Cary was in it for the game, he didn't like the idea of it being Isaac. Isaac didn't seem like the petty thief type. Of course everything about this way-too-easy-to-be-true job had thrown Cary off. Why not add one more weird detail to the mix?

"I'll look into him." In a little bit.

"Really do it, boss. If he's in there being sloppy, he could screw this up for both of us. You can't have him in your way."

"You're right, Jules. I'll deal with it."

"Today?"

"Tomorrow. It's nearly dinnertime. I don't want to get into it in front of Marigold. I'll get him alone tomorrow, catch him off guard. I'm supposed to be finishing up with the first part of my audit anyway."

"Is she really buying that it's taking this long?"

"I guess she's used to it. I haven't heard any protests, and I did tell her it would take a few days." Cary shrugged. "She has some seriously expensive shit and a hell of a lot of it. No wonder Isaac was tempted to sell it. If it even was him, which I seriously doubt."

"I have another question."

"What?"

"Do you really think he's her grandson?"

Cary was speechless again. He'd jumped to the thought of how the kid grew up with nothing, and the nice stuff might be tempting, put aside some cash in case things went sideways. He never even thought about... damn. Damn.

"He has to be. She'd recognize her own grandson. She's the one who came to him, isn't she? Besides, other people have tried this on her. She's never fallen for it before. He has to be the real thing."

"Or else—again—he's really good."

"If he was really good, he'd never be so sloppy to leave a trail. Sell while he's still in house."

"Everything doesn't always make sense. Just think about it, okay?"

"Yeah. I'm thinking."

CHAPTER 5

AFTER THE day he'd had—crazy but amazing, unexpected but somehow good, and Isaac refused for what had happened between them to be anything but good—dinner was nice and quiet. Marigold controlled herself mostly, making only a few really salacious remarks. Or perhaps she didn't want to, judging by the way she sat in her little armed chair like a queen and giggled every time she made some innuendo toward him or Cary that couldn't be brushed aside. Cary, for his part, was charming but not openly flirtatious toward Isaac. It was probably best that way. Isaac didn't want to embarrass himself by getting all blushy and googly-eyed in front of everyone like he'd been all day.

They never ate dinner at the big informal kitchen table where they had breakfast and sometimes lunch if enough people were around the house. It was either outside in the picturesque pergola, which featured fairy lights, outdoor mood music, and plush chairs, or in the dining room, which was high-ceilinged and plastered in gold with lots of heavy black wrought iron candle sconces and red accents. A little cliché Spanish if you asked Isaac, but he wasn't what you'd call a decorator. Everything was still so opulent to Isaac. He hadn't been in a bad way for a long time—the loft he'd shared with Roman was more than decent—but the heavy fabrics and shiny metals were overwhelmingly expensive, even to someone like him, who was around money all the time.

Marigold was her typical bubbly self, though, in the middle of the heaviness and the dim light. Kitty was as sweet and cheerful as she got, which meant she glared at him less than usual and refrained from making barbed comments all the way through the salad course. Cary, whom Isaac was trying not to maul over soup and flatbread, and Mike, who'd made an unconventional trip to the house for dinner, were on the opposite side of the huge wooden table from Isaac. It had been a hot day, and he supposed they were stuck in the dining room because the dusky heat of the pool deck was a little heavy for hot soup, salad, bread, and fajitas.

They'd all dressed not formally like he imagined they'd done in the days when Marigold was younger, but in nicer pants, button-ups, and dresses for Marigold and Kitty. Marigold had put on a huge gold necklace that engulfed her thin frame, and even wrapped a headband around her forehead. She looked beautiful in a faded, pale kind of way. Isaac couldn't help but be charmed by her. He'd been charmed by her from the start. He had to keep his eye on what he wanted, what he needed. The damn trust fund. It was really hard not to be romanced by the idea of Marigold as his grandmother, though, as much as he knew it was a bad idea to get in his head. He had to keep his eye on the prize.

"Cary, dear. Where are you from?" Marigold asked after she, Kitty, and Mike had done some pleasant chattering about the vineyard and the upcoming harvest.

Cary looked up from his soup starter. "Originally? Iowa. I've been based on the West Coast for a long time now. Since school ended."

Cary hadn't ever mentioned college. Isaac had a hard time seeing Cary cooped up in a classroom, although he spent half his workday cooped up with dusty old wines in a cellar. And probably in other people's old wine cellars, closets, and garages. Everywhere they kept random collections he had to deal with, catalog, authenticate. What a pain in the ass.

"What did you study in school?" she asked.

"Oh, history at Berkeley. I really loved the Bay Area, but I decided to settle up north. It was a cheaper place to start out in the end."

"Up north?"

"Portland, which worked out well since that's where our main office is."

Isaac got a twinge when he realized Cary lived nowhere near here or the loft he'd lived in with Roman in San Francisco. Or anywhere he could get to in an hour or so. Portland. Not far in the grand scheme of things, but it might as well be another country if you're trying to see someone. Isaac pinched himself under the table. *Knock it off. Yeah, not going to be ridiculous. The guy is fun to kiss. Not getting married any time soon.*

"And where do you usually work?"

"Actually, I get sent all over. My last job was in New York."

New York. Weird. Isaac had another jolt of familiar. He'd had quite a few of them with Cary, which was ridiculous. He'd never seen the guy before.

"Manhattan?"

"Yes. An heiress and her rare book collection. Very dusty." He grinned. "I had to call in an expert. I could only do auditing there too. I'd have no idea how to tell what any of those books are worth."

A book expert. Isaac shook it off. There were lots of expensive things in New York. Lots of expensive things everywhere, honestly.

"I've been to New York," Isaac said. "A few years ago."

"Did you like it?" Cary asked. His face was a mask of polite interest. But it was a mask. Isaac didn't know how he could tell, but that Cary wasn't the same one who'd pulled away from their kisses looking wrecked and horny and so involved in Isaac he could barely breathe. This was... yes. An act. Isaac wanted to grimace.

"It was too big, honestly. San Francisco is more my scene. Or somewhere even smaller. I didn't like how the buildings took up so much of the sky."

"It depends on what neighborhood you're in, I suppose. I quite like it there. But only in the fall and spring. New York winters are brutal."

"You prefer the rain?" Isaac smirked.

"I love the rain. You'd like it too, in my hometown, I think."

"Maybe I would." Maybe I wouldn't mind flying up there sometimes, spend the weekend in bed, hit the famous Portland food trucks. It sounded perfect.

Cary grinned at him. A real grin, like the kind Cary had gotten in the basement when the others weren't around. Isaac grinned back. He couldn't believe they were flirting in front of Marigold and the employees. Isaac knew it was dumb, but he couldn't seem to stop. He couldn't seem to stop leaning closer to Cary either, across the wide table until he could smell his soft cologne. Isaac remembered the hours of kissing earlier, and how much his body had strained for more. He wanted to lean over the table and take it. Kiss Cary until neither one of them could breathe. Not likely a good idea in this room. But tempting. So tempting.

"What are your plans for this evening?" Kitty asked Cary, She'd been much more conciliatory to him since her snap the other morning. It was really kind of weird to see her smile like that. It looked a little... reptilian? Like, he could tell it was supposed to be charming, but there was something off about Kitty. There always had been. He knew she didn't really like their handsome insurance rep. Not like Isaac did, at least. Probably not at all. She also probably didn't want Marigold to know that. There was no way Marigold couldn't see how fake her smile was.

"Oh, I don't have anything exciting planned. I have some paperwork to fill out, and I have a few bottles I've brought up from the basement. I have a few questions for the agent who did the last appraisal. I've found some inconsistencies."

"There aren't any problems, are there, dear?" Marigold raised her eyes.

"No. I'm sure not. Just some details that don't quite fit as far as I can tell. I'd like to talk to an expert."

"About which bottles?" Marigold looked concerned, but not overly so. "Maybe I can help you with that."

"Oh, it's nothing to worry about. There are a few individual bottles I'd like to double-check for age and authenticity. Then I want to do some more research on the Nine Sisters before I get to them. I've heard a few rumors circulating about that collection that I want to put to rest before I call it a done deal."

"I've never had any questions on those ones before…. Really?" Marigold looked perplexed.

"Yes. But like I said...." Cary smiled again, that big glamorous smile he seemed to save for people other than Isaac, which was weird. "I'm sure it's nothing to worry about. I'll know more after I fill in my paperwork and make some calls."

"If you're sure."

Cary leaned over and put his hand on Marigold's wrist. "I'll let you know more when I do."

His grandmother ate the rest of her soup, quieter than usual. He'd known Cary had some reservations about that one collection of wine, the sisters or whatever. He'd been a little iffy about them earlier in the cellars. Isaac had watched him earmark a few other bottles too. He guessed Cary was just being thorough at his job. He hoped Marigold, or whoever had bought those wines, hadn't been scammed. Isaac knew from experience it was easy to con someone into buying something they thought was priceless. Sell it for a smaller price than they think it's worth but a much bigger price than its real worth.

Then he realized the irony of what he was thinking.

I hope she wasn't scammed. Fucking hell. Really? Really? Isaac took a long moment to reevaluate what the fucking fuck he thought he was doing here.

It's different. I'm after money Marigold set aside for this grandkid who's probably dead. I'm not taking something that's hers. Only something nobody else was going to use. It's different.

Still. A part of him that wasn't trained to the hilt by Roman felt a little bad. Sometimes he slipped into the role of Isaac Shelley like he'd been doing it his whole life. In a way, he had. But it wasn't always easy. He had to pull out the awkward street kid he'd been when Roman found him—unsure of himself, unable to be in any sort of a relationship—and he had to remember how it felt not to know how to manipulate people into doing what he wanted. And then he had to act like that kid while convincing Marigold he was him, which was the weirdest and easiest part of this whole thing.

LATER THAT night, after everyone had gone to sleep, Isaac sat fidgeting in his room. He looked out the window at the pool, and the guesthouse that still had the lights on. He wasn't staring or anything; that would be creepy. Cary hadn't closed the blinds yet. Isaac didn't want to be creepy. But he wanted to be out there in the pool house for sure. He'd already taken off his dinner clothes and changed into a pair of light pajama bottoms and an old thin T-shirt. He thought about Cary in the guesthouse, maybe dressed in shorts and a tank top, golden skin, hair mussed, all sleepy and soft.

Damn it.

Isaac knew it was a bad idea. He also knew exactly what was going to happen if he walked down the stairs and across the pool deck. But fuck if he wasn't going to do it anyway.

He jammed his feet into an old pair of flip-flops and ran his fingers through his hair. It would have to do. Anything more would look like he was trying too hard. Which he was, but it wasn't good to look like it.

He crept down the backstairs and out the squeaky kitchen door. About halfway around the pool, he thought maybe he should turn around and go to bed, but he didn't. He kept walking until he found himself at the sliding door to the poolside guesthouse, knocking lightly. The lights were still on. Cary had to be awake.

Cary came around the corner where the closet and bathroom were. He looked happy and not all that surprised to see Isaac. He was wearing a pair of low-slung plaid bottoms and no shirt. Isaac's mouth went dry. Cary gestured for Isaac to come in.

"Hey. I was hoping I'd get to see you," he said after Isaac had entered, and slid the door closed behind him.

"Hi. Um, yeah. I couldn't stop thinking about today, and your lights were on."

"I was thinking about it too. You were distracting me from my work."

"Sorry?"

"Don't be sorry." Cary grinned. He reached out and tugged Isaac into his arms. "I wanted to kiss you some more."

"I'm okay with that."

Oh my God, that was cheesy. Quit talking. Just kiss him.

So he did. Isaac pulled Cary closer, just like he had about a million times earlier that day, and kissed him. Cary's skin, warm and golden just like Isaac had imagined, felt amazing squished up against his. Cary's hands sneaking under Isaac's shirt made him want to rip the damn thing off. Well, rip off everything, to be honest. He reached for the hem of his shirt and pulled it off. Maybe it was too soon. He didn't give a damn. He wanted Cary's skin on his.

They both shuddered when their chests met. Isaac could've sworn he felt something. Something electric between them.

"You smell good," Cary murmured. He nosed Isaac's neck and peppered his jawline with kisses.

Isaac moaned, swimming already in Cary's touch and the feel of his skin. "Hey, just to be clear," he murmured. "I want you."

Cary let out a low chuckle. "That was where I was hoping this was headed. I won't lie."

One, two, three more long, deep kisses and Isaac pulled away. "Is this when I ask what you're into?"

"It can be." He kissed and nibbled his way down Isaac's neck to his collarbone. "A little rough is fun but nothing too kinky. I'm sure you can tell I like kissing. A lot."

"Do you usually top?" Isaac felt like a moron for asking, but he had to know where this was going while he had at least a tiny bit of his head left intact.

Cary shrugged and sucked a rather deep mark into the joint where Isaac's neck met his shoulder. Isaac shivered hard. "Whatever feels right at the time. I'm happy with both."

"F-fuck. Good. Me too. Both."

Cary slid his hands down the back of Isaac's loose sleep pants and dragged his nails lightly up the sides of his cheeks. Nobody had ever done that to him before. It made his knees buckle.

"Wanna lie down?" Cary asked.

Isaac gulped. Hell, yes. He didn't reply, simply backed up step by step across the room until his knees bent and he fell onto the plush bed. Cary toppled over him. They laughed and kissed, worming their way all the way onto the bed until their toes were no longer hanging off the side.

"I keep wanting to touch your skin. It's so soft," Cary murmured. He trailed his lips down Isaac's chest. Isaac wound his fingers in Cary's hair and tugged on it when Cary got closer to the waistband of his pajamas.

"C'mere," he muttered and pulled Cary back up for more kisses. "Not done with this part yet."

Cary didn't seem to have any complaint. He crawled up between Isaac's legs and lowered himself, pressing Isaac into the mattress. "I told you I liked kissing," he said, before sinking into another breathless kiss. He pulled Isaac's hands over his head, wound their fingers together, and rolled his hips hard, grinding against Isaac's growing cock.

Isaac decided then and there he was going to have dreams about this night for months. He lifted his thighs and wrapped them around Cary's lean hips. Cary ground down again, and this time Isaac met him in the middle. They moaned into kisses and squeezed each other's fingers, panted, and kissed and sucked love bites into each other's necks. Isaac wanted more, even if he could barely handle what he already had.

"I wanna be naked," he said. "You too."

"Damn, kid. Okay."

Cary let go of Isaac's hands and rolled aside. He lifted his hips and pulled his loose bottoms off, tossing them over the side of the bed. Isaac had been in the middle of tugging his drawstring open when he froze to stare at Cary's body. It was exactly what Isaac had pictured: long and leanly muscled, covered in golden skin, lightly furred legs, pretty darkening cock curved up toward his belly. Fucking beautiful. Jesus, he wanted to touch and taste it all. He didn't even know where to start.

"Hey. You too," Cary said softly.

"Sorry," Isaac forced out through a suddenly lust-dry mouth. "Got distracted. You're so fucking hot."

"Lemme help."

Cary shooed Isaac's hands away and pulled his drawstring open. He slid his hands back into Isaac's pants and pushed them down and off. "Hi, pretty."

Isaac blushed, if that was even possible with his entire body already so hot for Cary he could barely do anything other than touch. He reached for Cary the second his pants were tossed aside. He had to get to that skin and hair and his amazing kisses. He wanted those back immediately. They slid together on a satisfied sigh, legs twining, hearts pounding against each other's chests.

"This is kinda crazy, huh?" Isaac said softly. He'd messed around with guys before, at least a few times, but nothing had ever been so consuming. It had only been one day. How could he want this so much already? It didn't matter how. The truth was there in his racing pulse and his hard cock. He wanted Cary, and he wanted him badly.

"Mmhmmm." Cary didn't say anything else. He dove in for more kisses. "Hey," he finally said. "So I want to take this slow and touch and kiss you and all that stuff but—"

"Next time." Isaac wanted it too intensely to wait.

"Yeah?"

"Yes." And then he realized he was probably not very experienced for a reason. Someday he'd learn how to act like the adult he was supposed to be. "Shit. You have anything with you?"

Cary grinned. "Yeah. Not even a habit, but I guess it's a good thing I stuck them in my bag this time, right?"

Isaac nodded. His throat was dry. This was really going to happen. He watched Cary slide off the bed and lope over to his duffel bag, warm-skinned and lion-sleek. The man really was beautiful. He dug around for a few moments and returned, victorious, with a small bottle of lube and a handful of condoms, which he tossed aside.

"I've gotta get my mouth on you first," Cary said. "That seriously needs to happen, like, now. Okay?"

Isaac nodded. How could he not? Cary flopped gracefully onto his belly between Isaac's thighs and ran his palms up the insides of them. "Your skin is so soft. I just want to mark it up."

Isaac touched Cary's hair for a moment, unsure if it would be okay. Cary nuzzled his head into Isaac's hands. Cary must've liked it. Isaac tried to ignore the warmth spreading in his belly and bit his lip to keep from grinning. He threaded his fingers lightly through Cary's hair and tugged. Cary moaned. He mouthed up Isaac's shaft and sucked it down.

"Holy… ohmygod." Isaac had to keep his hips from bucking up into the warmth of Cary's mouth. As it was he was seriously in danger of losing it before anything even started. Just the sight of him, gorgeous pink lips stretched around Isaac's cock, was too much. Isaac squeezed his eyes closed and leaned back onto the duvet. He couldn't watch. That would be the end of him. He had to concentrate on the sensations, on the wet heat and the way Cary's tongue knew just where to massage.

Cary's hands had slipped around Isaac's cheeks and were getting closer and closer to where Isaac wanted them.

Isaac took a deep breath, tried to grasp some tiny little bit of control, and blindly reached around for the little pile of condoms Cary dropped on the bedside table. He grabbed one and slammed it down on the duvet. Then he found the bottle of lube and put it right next to them.

"Please. Inside, now."

Cary lifted his head. His lips were slick and gorgeous. He looked like some sort of debauched angel. "You sure?"

Isaac nearly laughed. "Very sure." He nudged the lube toward Cary with his calf.

Cary unclicked the cap before reaching between Isaac's cheeks.

"You okay with this way?" Isaac felt a dry thumb press against his rim. Yes. Jesus Christ, he was okay with it.

"I like it. Yeah."

"Good. But I'll definitely want to feel this inside me later." He ran another exploratory finger up Isaac's cock. It was so hard and wet, that little touch nearly sent him off. He gripped the sheets.

"Now. Please."

Cary slicked up his fingers and then brought them back to play with Isaac, tease him to the point where he was about to go insane. "You know," Cary said casually. "This would be better for you with my mouth. I'd love to taste you."

"You can't say shit like that if you don't want me to come like right now," Isaac groaned.

"What if I do this?" Cary sank two fingers in, slow and slick.

Isaac grabbed Cary's shoulder and keened. "Yes." It was exactly what he needed.

Cary worked him slowly, added another finger, kissed his neck, sucked his nipples. He had Isaac about to lose his mind by the time he pulled out his fingers gently.

"You ready?"

Isaac spread his legs and canted his hips toward Cary. He tugged on his cock desperately. He needed to feel something so bad. Cary had him about to explode. "Fuck me. Please."

"Jesus."

Cary made quick work of sliding on a condom and slicking himself up. "Scoot down here. Closer."

Isaac moved so quickly, they nearly collided. Cary chuckled and leaned in for a kiss. "Tell me when you're good, okay?" He whispered against Isaac's lips, then started to push in.

He took it slow, agonizing inches at a time. Isaac wanted to cry out and kick at the bedsheets. He satisfied himself by wrapping his legs around Cary's hips and pulling. Isaac needed more before he was going to fucking pass out.

"I'm okay. I'm good. Move." He slammed one hand against the wall and the other he used to grab at Cary's ass, pulling him as close as he could.

"So hot, babe. You're gorgeous." Cary started to roll his hips, deep and slow, grinding in so hard Isaac saw stars. It was full and thick inside him, pressure and pulling and fucking hell holy shit. Isaac had been into it before, but now he was about to explode. Cary had found his spot and was on it relentlessly, hitting it hard with every stroke.

"There?"

Isaac couldn't speak. He could only nod and grab at Cary even harder.

They were quiet for a long time after that. He didn't think either of them was capable of more than monosyllables, grunts, and hard breathing. Isaac knew he was getting close. It had never happened so fast before. The feeling was intense, rushing him, pulling him over. Cary hadn't even touched his cock once.

"Cary. I'm gonna—"

"Yes. Now."

Cary wriggled a hand between them and wrapped it around Isaac. One pull, and he was gone. His vision blacked out and he arched off the bed, but he barely remembered doing it. All he could do was shout.

Cary flopped to the side and breathed hard. Isaac felt his ribs going in and out, heard his exhausted exhales. He wasn't quite ready to process something as complicated as breathing yet. All he could do was float, giddy, on his body high. He didn't know how long it would take to come down. It had to be the best thing he'd ever felt. Isaac heard Cary rustling around a little bit before lying down. A warm hand found his, threading their fingers together. Isaac squeezed.

"Fuck that was… fuck." Isaac didn't know if his higher brain function had returned yet. He was guessing no. His mind was on constant loops of *Caryhotmorenowjesusfuck*. Probably not quite ready to speak in actual sentences yet.

"Yeah, fuck." Apparently neither was Cary. "I can't…."

"Me neither." Isaac laughed weakly, only slightly alarmed by the goo in his brain and the fact that he didn't want to do anything but lie there and let his body thrum away happily.

"So rest and then try that again?" Cary asked breathlessly.

All of a sudden, Isaac's body was ready for action. Imagine that. "I'll be good in a few minutes."

Cary barked out a loud laugh and rolled over on top of Isaac, sticky, sweaty skin and all. "Okay, youngling. Your turn to show me what you've got."

CHAPTER 6

CARY FELT weirdly guilty that morning when he woke up to a sleep-rumpled Isaac on the other side of his bed. In a way, it was exactly what he'd wanted. Everything was going according to plan. Isaac was primed. They'd gotten close, he knew Cary was worried about the wines, he was ready to sell Cary's general authenticity to Marigold. Everything was going perfectly. But he felt guilty. Yes, Cary Talbot felt guilty. It was such an uncommon feeling he didn't recognize it at first. But there it was, sitting heavy and uncomfortable in his gut.

And then there was Jules and her warning about the stolen fenced items, which he'd still not done anything about. More guilt.

Sure, there hadn't been much of a chance to deal with it, but he hadn't really put much effort into finding a chance either. It involved a lot of work getting to Sandro if he wanted to talk to him in person. Burner phones and complicated dead drops, perfect for the paranoid and on the run, and he really didn't have the time for the whole song and dance. He'd probably make a "research" day of it soon, supposedly look up the wines, set up a fake authentication, get Sandro and Marigold's hocked goods squared away.

Deal with Isaac.

Weirdest part was he didn't want Isaac to be stealing from Marigold. It had taken Cary even longer to realize that than to realize he was feeling guilty. All these emotions. So annoying. But they were real, and there was no use denying it. He didn't want Isaac to be wise enough to know the best fences and the quickest ways to get rid of stolen goods. He wanted Isaac to be the street kid with the squishy soft heart who was so obviously in love with his new grandmother. He wanted Isaac Shelley to be real. And that's what worried Cary the most.

"Morning." Isaac rolled over and opened his eyes. His dark hair was fluffed up funny on one side. He was milk-pale even at the end of summer, with only a dusting of freckles and residual faint gold to show he'd seen the sun. His eyes were huge and soft, and his mouth like every dream about kissing Cary had ever had. He was beautiful. Perfect. He was going to be a pain in Cary's ass, wasn't he? And his conscience.

"Good morning to you. How are you feeling?"

Isaac stretched a little. "Kinda sore. We didn't exactly take it easy last night." He blushed. "Good, though. Like. It was so worth it."

"It was." Cary rolled Isaac into his arms and touched his pale skin. He'd touched for hours the night before. Touched everywhere he could. Kissed and licked until he'd nearly made Isaac scream. It had been almost dawn when they'd passed out, pink-skinned and damp from a very necessary shower. Touching Isaac really should've lost its appeal by now. Somehow, it had only grown more appealing.

"So. Um, what are you up to today? Please tell me not another day in the cellar."

"I really should get down there. I don't have much left. Maybe a day and a half tops."

"So come out with me in the morning and do that in the afternoon when it's awful and hot."

"Come out with you?" Cary raised his eyebrows. Isaac smiled at him, somehow both sleepy and enthusiastic. It made Cary want to kiss him. Which seemed to be his typical response to everything Isaac did.

"Yes. You haven't seen the whole vineyard yet. It's beautiful. We can take out a couple of Marigold's horses. I have a bit of a knack with them."

"You think you'll be up to ride a horse?" Cary asked with a small smirk.

"You think you will be?"

Isaac returned what he took twofold. That much was certain. In lots of ways. Cary gave himself a moment or two to stretch experimentally and smiled back.

"Yeah. Despite our rather strenuous efforts, I think I should be just fine."

That's how he ended up, nearly an hour later, on the back of a pretty, glossy mare named Cinnamon, who was the color of a redhead and just about as feisty—at least if he was going by his ex, Kelly. She could've given Jules a run for her money.

"You sure you want to ride Cinnamon? She's not exactly a beginner's horse. I can always give you Cupcake."

As if Cary was going to be caught dead on a goddamn horse named Cupcake. She had a pink mane. Pink. "I think I'm okay." Isaac giggled. "Who on earth dyed the poor thing's mane that ungodly color, though? It's so wrong."

"Marigold. She wanted Cupcake to look like a rock star. It's kind of cute with her white body, right?"

"It's an affront to nature."

Isaac laughed out loud at that. "It'll come out in a few washes. Cupcake doesn't seem to mind. She's such a sweetie."

Unlike Cinnamon, who seemed to have it in her mind to take off running at the slightest provocation.

"You sure you're okay?"

Cary was fine, damn it. He wasn't exactly propped on top of his horse like he belonged there, like Mister Pretty Pants over there on his Arabian, who was named Caramel. Cary wanted to know who'd named the damn horses. He felt for their dignity.

"I'm totally fine. Let's go."

Cinnamon was antsy for the first few minutes, but they got used to each other, and then she was happy prancing behind Caramel while Isaac wound through disgustingly pretty green squares filled with neat rows of grape vines. The air smelled sweet, like ripening plump fruit on the vine, green, sun, and earth. Cary thought that if someone had told him a month ago he'd be trotting through a vineyard on a horse named Cinnamon, he might have punched them. With a charming smile, of course.

"How long until harvest?"

"Not long," Isaac said. "I'm just getting to know how everything works around here, but Mike said harvest will start in a couple of weeks. I guess the crop was really good this year. I don't even know if crop is the right word." Isaac shrugged. "I really am a newbie. I'm sure I say fifty things a day that make Kitty cringe."

Everyone probably made the frosty princess cringe. "I don't know how I feel about her," Cary said.

"I know how I feel about her." Isaac rolled her eyes. "Pretty sure those feelings are mutual. She doesn't seem to like me much."

"Why not?"

"Guess she doesn't trust me. Some guy with no memory earlier than fourteen shows up claiming to be Marigold's grandson? I wouldn't trust me either."

"But you didn't show up. Didn't Marigold find you in a restaurant and recognize you? You weren't pulling the same game everyone else did."

Isaac started for a moment, then relaxed in his saddle with a shrug. "I guess Kitty doesn't think that's a good enough reason to think I'm not scamming her."

"You okay?" Cary asked

"Yeah. Just... I don't know. Tired of trying to prove who I am when I have no idea. I know Kitty thinks I'm playing games with Marigold. I bet half the other people in this town do too."

Cary grinned. "I don't blame them. The lost heir is the oldest con in the book. Literally. At least one of them. People like these guys who have money must have missing relatives coming out of the cracks looking for payouts all the time."

"How do you know that?"

Cary shrugged. "It's just how it is. You work in insurance, you see people trying to pull that trick all the time."

"And one I'd be dumb to follow their lead. I really don't have a clue who I was when I was a kid. I grew up on the streets and I really was just as freaked out as anyone else would be when Marigold pulled me aside and started assuring me I was her grandson. All of that is true. It was the weirdest day in my life."

"I bet it was."

Cary had a hard time reconciling the confusion on Isaac's face with the person who could set up something that complex and that dumb—get himself into the house and gain Marigold's trust only to start stealing and hocking goods. He thought he'd learned to spot them in his life. Maybe this kid was the best. Maybe he wasn't stealing from Marigold after all. Cary determined he'd figure that out after their ride. And the rest of the cataloging. And maybe a few more kisses.

"IT'S ALWAYS so chilly down here." Isaac shivered. His skin was pale but a little sun-kissed from their morning on the horses. Cary was sore; he'd been sore since he woke up that morning, but it had been a good kind of sore then. That had turned to an aching, painful kind of sore after a few hours of working in the wine cellar. He wanted to curl up in the huge sunny bed in his guesthouse with Isaac and take a long nap.

I still need to check him out....

He'd ignored Jules's warning the night before. He didn't *want* to check Isaac out. Of course he was a fool if he didn't, so he would. Eventually. Isaac had the potential to screw everything up for Cary if he was the culprit and he made any really dumb choices and someone noticed. Once people started to look for trouble, they didn't exactly stop at the first thing they found.

"I know. It is cold down here. I wouldn't mind doing the rest of this out by the pool." Cary chuckled.

"We're almost done, aren't we?"

Cary had even had Isaac helping him make notes of things, bottles checked, inconsistencies, ones he had "questions" about. It made Isaac more invested, and made Cary look more likely to be really doing his job and not trying to pull something. Not that anyone had a reason to doubt him.

"I could warm you up," Isaac added.

Cary giggled, and not even on purpose. "You really just said that?"

"Hey. I'm not exactly Don Juan."

"I don't mind. It's cute." Cary liked Isaac just the way he was. He was painfully embarrassed by how much.

"Great. Cute. That's exactly what every twenty-four-year-old guy wants to be. Next you're going to say adorable."

"Like a little, big-eyed puppy."

"Screw you."

Cary leaned forward and whispered in Isaac's ear, just to see how much he could make him shiver. "I think you took care of that for at least half of last night. I'd be happy to do it some more if you weren't satisfied with the results."

It worked. Isaac's whole body erupted in shivers, and he gripped the laptop he'd been holding. "You can't do that kind of stuff if we're going to stay down here and work like adults."

"Instead of making out like… not adults?"

Isaac shrugged. "It's not exactly helping you get out of here when I spend half the time with my tongue in your mouth."

"I'm not complaining." Cary took the laptop out of Isaac's hand and put it down. "C'mere."

Kissing. Yes. They were going to do more of that. Mostly because Cary wanted to. He didn't need it for his scheme anymore. Isaac was exactly where he wanted him to be. In more ways than one. He didn't need to be romanced anymore. Isaac curled around Cary's body like he was meant to be there, his arms slid around Cary's neck, his thigh rested against Cary's hips. He just… fit. Annoyingly perfect fit too. And then there were his lips. They slotted into Cary's like they'd been doing it for years instead of a couple of days. He moaned into Cary's mouth and went for it, kissing with innocent enthusiasm and more skill than he had any right to have acquired. It was intoxicating and probably crazy. It was perfect.

Cary kissed back, winding his fingers into Isaac's wild dark hair, nipping at his lush bottom lip. He moaned too, and ran his hand up under Isaac's shirt to feel his skin. He couldn't get enough of his skin.

"Jesus," Isaac finally muttered. "How am I going to stop kissing you long enough for you to finish here?"

"I don't know. I don't want to finish. That means I'd have to leave."

Cary hadn't even meant to say that. But it was true. It was very true. He wanted to stay in the idyllic perfect place and kiss Isaac forever.

What the everlasting fuck?

That thought was enough to bring him to his senses. Jesus. Cary needed to get his job done and get the hell out. Immediately, before he did something stupid like go shopping for pretty ring-shaped gold things. Unfortunately, jobs like this one required time. Delicacy. Things he'd just decided he no longer had. He was screwed. Like actually royally screwed, and he'd done it to himself.

Cary decided what he needed was to get out that night. Talk to Jules. Hang out somewhere outside this damn house with this damn boy who was doing things to mess with his mind. Yes. That would do it.

"I don't want you to finish either. It's, I don't know, childish of me but I just want to be near you all the time. I probably sound like a stupid kid right now, but I do. I don't...." Isaac sounded like he didn't know what to say. But Cary knew what the answer was. Say nothing. Kiss Isaac some more and then get to the goddamned wines. Emotional dialogue wasn't going to get him anywhere other than in huge trouble. He had to turn his timetable up a little. Get to the part where he got them to believe the Nine Sisters were fake. Cut to the damn chase. That's what he had to do. Cary shook it off and went for his game face.

"One more kiss, then work?" He turned his best smile on Isaac.

Isaac's smile faltered a little. "One more kiss."

Cary leaned over and kissed Isaac soft, then deeper. It was obvious Isaac wasn't as into it as he'd been before. Cary didn't understand.

"What's wrong?" he asked.

"I just… I don't like your professional smile. It's not you."

What? "What do you mean?" Nobody ever knew when Cary was charming them on purpose. He was too good for that. What the hell?

"I can tell when you're being, like, intentionally charming. It looks fake. I can also tell when you're smiling because you want to. That smile looks real."

Cary had spent years perfecting his act. To have one kid, who, yes, was from the streets and probably lived on his ability to know when people were trying to pull one over on him, but still. To have that kid be able to see through it so easily sucked. And it made him mad.

"I'm not being fake."

"Cary." Clearly Isaac knew better. *Clearly* Cary needed to work on that.

"Let's get going on these wine bottles. There are quite a few of them left, and I don't want to be down here forever."

He pulled away and went to the rack where they'd left off the day before. Only a little bit of warm-up work left, a deceptively thorough fake report, a few more seeds to plant, and then it was time. He took the top left bottle out and started to examine it. A warm weight wrapped around him from behind.

"What did I do?" Isaac asked.

"Nothing. Just, fuck. You were right. I spooked myself by how much I want to spend time with you, gave you a practiced smile, and you were fucking right. Nobody ever sees it, and you saw it."

Cary couldn't believe he'd just told the truth. He'd said exactly what he was feeling, and he hadn't spontaneously burst into flame. Not yet at least. Telling people how he felt was something Cary avoided at all costs. Obviously. He needed to get away from one gorgeous Isaac Shelley.

"Don't you think it's because I know you?"

Cary gave Isaac a look. The thought of someone other than Jules knowing him was… unsettling.

Isaac shrugged. "Okay, I know we just met. But sometimes, don't you meet someone and you feel like you know them already? There's something about them that makes them familiar before they even talk? It was like that for me with you."

That worried Cary. That Isaac could see so easily through the con to see when he was being real. That meant he had to play it really carefully when it got to the Nine Sisters. If Isaac knew when he was lying, he had to make sure his paperwork and whoever Jules hired to authenticate the damn wines was perfect. Fucking perfect. And he had to figure out why exactly this kid had his number. Nobody else ever had.

"I get it. I'm not usually all that good at reading people, but it seems like you are. I'm sorry."

Isaac turned Cary around and cupped his face. They were nearly the same height. Cary both liked and hated the fact that Isaac could stare at him so easily. Peel back his layers like that. "Don't worry about it. Kiss me."

This time, the kiss was real and tangible. It was tongues and tastes and zero hesitation. Cary sank into Isaac's mouth and into the kiss like the past few minutes never happened. He was still spooked. Hell, he was going to be spooked for a long time. Until he got the hell out of here with his wines and his sanity. But he could do this. He was good. He'd always been good. He could do it. It was just going to be a challenge.

They passed another hour, kissing and cataloging wines. Cary picked a few more to be wary of, just so that when it came to the end, he didn't look like he was singling out the sisters and passing everything else through no problem. He had Isaac make notes and take photos of the labels and took a lot of kissing breaks. More and more, sometimes after each bottle they started, kissing until they were out of breath and laughing.

"We're never going to get this done at this rate," Isaac muttered. "Not that I'm really unhappy about that."

"We're nearly there. Just need to do the reserve area." Cary gestured over to where a locked wrought iron gate protected the racks of Marigold's most expensive liquid treasures. Most people could see those wines from a distance but not touch. It was where the sisters were. And everything else Marigold was most concerned about. He had the key and his laptop, and he could fucking do this. Cary tried not to think too hard about the sheer worth of what was behind that one antique gate. If he were Marigold, he'd have a hell of a lot more than a simple lock to guard it. Sure, there was a key-code entry at the top of the stairs to the cellar itself, but even that was quite simple to crack. Cary decided he'd have to talk to Marigold about that before he left. Just because he was stealing from her didn't mean he wanted other people to do it.

"One more kiss before we move to that section?" Isaac asked.

"One more kiss."

Cary leaned forward again and nipped at Isaac's bee-stung lips. He delved into a kiss that seemed more like a prelude to something else and not just a simple kiss like the rest of them had been that morning. He wanted to spread Isaac out on his bed again, or maybe even the big table down here in the wine cellar, and taste all the parts he hadn't gotten to the night before. He couldn't wait for later. He hoped they got to play again. He wound his fingers into Isaac's hair and pulled. Isaac let out a low moan.

"Excuse me?"

Cary leapt backward, and Isaac's face stained in a horrified blush. Kitty.

"Um, pardon me." Cary tried to be suave about it. Wasn't easy when Isaac looked like he was about to melt into the ground. "We'll just go over to the reserve area."

"I apologize for that," Kitty said.

Why the hell is she—oh shit.

And that's when Cary realized they had other company. Even better. She already hated him, and she was about to hate him even more for embarrassing her in front of whomever she was with.

"It's okay." He didn't recognize the other woman with Kitty, but she didn't seem to be offended. In fact, she was smirking into her hand like she was trying not to giggle. "I'll just follow you."

Kitty nodded briskly. She looked quite a bit more pleasant than she ever did when she was dealing with Isaac or Cary. He imagined she was a customer. "As you can see, Falling River isn't just a working winery. Marigold Shelley, the owner, keeps a collection of rare and historical wines here at her residence. We typically open this area for enthusiasts to tour, but we've been closed down for an insurance inspection this week."

Cary thought the other woman might have snickered at the word *inspection*. He would've, too, if he weren't more embarrassed than he'd been in a long, long time, getting caught making out in the basement. There really was something about Isaac that brought out the teenager in him.

"Marigold has quite the collection. Bottles from around the world, some dating back to our country's first president." Kitty led her guest around the racks, pulling certain bottles and discussing them.

"This one," he heard her saying, "is a rare Bordeaux from the mid nineteenth century. Historians say it's the same kind Edgar Allen Poe liked to drink when he was writing. Marigold has always been a huge fan, so she had to find a bottle. It wasn't an easy task, but we managed. It's one of the prizes in her collection."

"Can I see the Nine Sisters?" the woman asked. "I've heard so many rumors. I just want to see if they really exist."

"Rumors?" Kitty asked.

Jules. Cary knew it then. This woman wasn't a buyer. She was a fucking plant, and Jules was a genius. He wanted to do a jig all over Kitty's sour face.

"Yes, I've heard a few collections have surfaced over the years that were supposed to be the Nine Sisters but turned out to be frauds. Some current experts believe they never really existed, and it was just a story told to show that Portugal approved of George Washington and the fledgling nation."

"I assure you that Mrs. Shelley's Nine Sisters are very real. They've been in the family for years. Since prohibition."

Bad wording. Cary knew that whoever Jules had hired could work with that.

"You mean these bottles were procured during the time when… having alcohol was illegal and people were making counterfeit bottles in dark basements all over the region? Including this one?" The woman raised her eyes. Cary knew Isaac was listening hard. He was too. She was a good actor.

"Yes. But they've been authenticated many times since."

"By whom?"

"The wine experts that Falling River has worked with for years." Again. Not the best answer. Kitty seemed to catch her own mistake. "Fully accredited, I assure you."

"I'm sure. I'd like to see them please."

Kitty pulled a ring of keys off of her belt. "They're over here."

She led the woman over to where Cary and Isaac were standing. "If you please," Kitty said. She shook her keys, and Cary took the hint and got out of the way. Kitty unlocked the door and pulled it open.

THAT NIGHT at dinner, Cary's phone buzzed as he was finishing up his ice cream. He hadn't meant to leave the phone in his pocket. This wasn't the kind of house where answering calls at the dinner table was acceptable.

"I apologize," he muttered and pulled his phone out to silence it. He looked quickly at the message.

sos. call me — j

Jules had found something else. Great. Cary slid his phone back into his pocket.

Isaac gave him an inquisitive look. "Everything okay?"

Cary nodded. "I think so. That was my assistant at the main office. She found something she really wants me to take a look at."

Marigold chuckled. "Why is she still at work?"

"She's a bit of a workaholic. I think she's going to get promoted soon. I'll be sorry to see her go."

Jules wasn't going anywhere, Cary hoped. But he did want to promote her, if there were such things as promotions in their odd little company. He'd been sharing pretty generously with her, cutting most takes 60/40 and barely charging her rent. But she'd had some ideas for cons they could do without a single person other than her running the tech. He wanted to unclip her wings and let her fly on a few of them. It was just hard sometimes to let go of the control.

"Good at her job?" Marigold asked.

"Very." Which was more than true. She was amazing at her job. It was just a very different job than Marigold assumed, obviously.

"I'm glad. Back when I was a girl, there were very few of us in any business."

"I didn't know you worked, Grandmother," Isaac said.

Marigold smiled. "I didn't come from a place like this, but I knew I wanted to end up in one. Marrying your grandfather was a happy accident. I figured I'd have to work for it."

Cary heard something in her tone. She wasn't quite telling the truth. He wondered if Isaac heard it as well or if his psychic powers only stretched to Cary himself. Probably. Convenient and all that.

"That's amazing. I don't know what I would've done if I'd been you."

"I imagine the same thing."

Okay, she really was not saying something. Cary looked at her inquisitively for a moment, but then looked away. He finished the last few bites of his ice cream and waited for the others to finish as well before he pushed his chair back.

"If you don't mind, I'll go and return Jules's call. It seemed rather urgent."

Isaac looked at him questioningly. He couldn't exactly ask if he was going to spend the night in Cary's guesthouse. Not in front of an entire room full of people. Cary tried to nod imperceptibly. He didn't think it would take Jules too long to tell him whatever it was she needed to tell him. He wanted Isaac there that night.

"Have a good evening, dear. I hope it doesn't take too long," Marigold said. Intentionally or not, she'd just given him the perfect opportunity to tell Isaac the same thing.

"Oh, it'll be a short call, I imagine. I'll probably just spend the rest of the night relaxing."

He caught Isaac's eye after everyone else returned to their conversation. He'd gotten it. Cary smiled.

He walked around the pool, enjoying the warm night air, and slid the glass door of the guesthouse open. It was warm inside, but he didn't dare have his conversation with the door open. He'd have to save that for when he was finished. He pulled up his contacts and tapped on Jules's name. The phone rang a few times before she picked it up, breathless.

"Hey, I have news."

"Bad? Good? Did our usual authenticator fall through? I don't really feel like bribing another one."

"No. That's all taken care of. It's Isaac. Another one of Marigold's necklaces popped up. This time there's a picture of the item and a signature. Isaac sold it, Cary. He's the one who signed it over."

"He'd never do that."

"If he's just a scared kid trying to get money, he might be stupid enough. There's a signature there. Sandro messaged me a picture of the item and the slip."

"Send it to me." Cary felt an annoying swoop in his belly, the kind that told him he hadn't wanted Isaac to be stealing from his grandmother. At least he wasn't going to have to look into it much if they had proof. "If you can e-mail it to me, that would be great. I'll print it out. I need something to show him. I'm going to have to tell him to back off."

"Are you sure you want to show your cards?"

"I might have to. Let me think about how I want to play this. He has to stop. Somehow I need to get that across to him."

"It's risky, boss. This whole job is giving me the willies. I really think you should pull out of there."

"You've been saying that since the moment I got here."

"And I've been meaning it exactly that long as well. I think you should get out."

"I think I can make it work." Cary was nothing if not stubborn when it came to a good payoff. That's exactly what he was going to do on this one. Be stubborn. He wanted those damn wines, and he'd already nearly gotten marooned on a back road in wine country, shared his damn feelings with someone. No. He was seeing this one through.

"Is that really why you're staying?"

Cary felt a burst of irritation. If it was so obvious Jules could feel it through the phone, then he'd lost more than he thought. "Yes. That's why I'm staying." He didn't want to go into it. Didn't want to think about how Isaac's kiss had been with him all day, even when their lips weren't close.

"If that's what you say, boss. Just be careful. You're getting your heart into this one for some reason, and we all know what happens when that messy can is opened up."

"People get caught. It's fine, Jules. I have this. If nothing else, she doesn't buy it, I'm out some plane fare, and we find something in the Bay Area to make up our costs. I want to see this through, though. It's… important. I'm not walking away from this one."

"Just be careful around the kid. We don't know what he's up to."

"Other than sticky fingers. Yeah. I got it. Careful."

Cary hung up and flopped on his bed, where he waited for the e-mail that Jules had promised him. He should've expected it. Cary was rarely the only person pulling a scam in any given city. He was just disappointed.

CHAPTER 7

ISAAC DIDN'T know why he bothered to sneak out of Cary's room and shower in his own. It was useless to pretend he hadn't been there all night. Marigold knew what was going on between the two of them, and he didn't really care what anyone else thought. She was the one who would eventually sign his papers, not Kitty. The others seemed pretty oblivious to him and Cary. The only disapproving stares he'd gotten came from Kitty's quarter, and that was nothing new. He'd resigned himself to the fact that she was going to disapprove of him no matter what he did. Luckily for him, it didn't seem like Marigold was paying her much attention any longer.

Still, Isaac tiptoed across the pool deck in the early, early morning on his way to the kitchen door, where he planned to tiptoe just as quietly up the backstairs to his bedroom.

He pulled the door to the kitchen open and winced when it squeaked a little. Unfortunately he could've been mostly silent, and Marigold would still have been sitting there with a cup of tea. He jumped, and then she jumped and spilled a little down her sleeve.

"Damn it!" She wiped at it, laughing.

"Sorry, I didn't mean to scare you," Isaac murmured.

"No, I imagine you meant to do the walk of shame up the backstairs. Darling, you're an adult. I don't mind if you're spending time with Cary. He's a handsome man."

Isaac couldn't believe how cool she was being. Knowing was one thing, witnessing the aftermath all over his neck at five in the morning was another. "I know. I just... don't want to be disrespectful."

"You're not disrespecting me. Go get some more sleep, dear. Nobody should be up this early. If I hadn't woken, I wouldn't be either."

"Thank you, Grandmother. I'll see you at breakfast."

He showered and slid into his bed, which he hadn't seen in a few nights. It was still cushy and comfortable, better than any bed he'd had before, but there was something missing, and he couldn't believe it was Cary. How could Cary, after only a few short nights, be part of what made him comfortable enough to fall asleep? No. He refused to think it, which of course didn't work at all. Isaac wondered what he should do about it. Cary was nearly done. He'd be leaving Falling River soon, and Isaac hopefully after him unless something went awry with his plans. Isaac didn't think he'd see him again. Unless he managed to get Cary's number... which Cary hadn't offered. Or asked for from Isaac either. Isaac made a plan to try.

It was a few hours later when he walked into the breakfast room, dressed, somewhat chipper, and only a tad embarrassed still at being caught walk of shaming by his not-real step-grandmother, who sent him an awfully conspiratorial smile. Isaac blushed.

"Morning, everyone."

"Morning," Marigold said innocently, like they hadn't spoken a few hours previous. Everyone else echoed it.

"What are you up to today?" he asked her.

"Actually, my plan is to scour the house. I'm missing one of my favorite necklaces, and I'd really like to get it back. I've had it for years."

"Is it valuable or just like... sentimental?" Isaac asked. He'd hate for Marigold to lose something that was worth something to her personally.

"It's both. Your grandfather bought it for me, and he liked his trinkets to be on the spendy side. But mostly it has a lot of sentimental value. We hadn't been married very long when he bought that for me. We were in Paris, and it was a lovely romantic trip. I'd really just like it back, and I hope it's not lost forever."

"What does it look like?" Cary asked.

"It's gold, with flowers in gold and platinum, and then some flowers also in diamonds and sapphires. It's cocktail length." She looked at Mike's perplexed face. "Longer. I can put it over my head without undoing a clasp."

Mike nodded.

"Were you wearing that at dinner the day I got here? That sounds familiar," Cary said. "The stones were super clear. I remember that one. I have an eye for sapphires."

"I was, actually. Good memory, dear."

Isaac cocked his head to the side. He'd heard Cary say the word sapphires before. He knew it, he just didn't know when. It was one of those moments he'd had a few times where Cary seemed familiar, and not just from the past few days, but from… before. Like back when Isaac was still with Roman. Where on earth could he have run into Cary before? It seemed nearly impossible. They existed in completely different circles, and he'd have been sure to remember if Roman or he had ever dealt with insurance auditors before. Cons tended to remember that. Especially when they looked like Cary and had the potential to get people like Isaac and Roman very arrested.

"I'll keep my eye open for it," Cary said. "Not that I expect to be anywhere where the necklace should turn up. You might try scarves or the shirt you were wearing. Both of those tend to snag jewelry."

"Good idea, dear. I'll try those first."

Cary pushed his chair back after he downed his last bite of the amazing breakfast scramble Gretchen had made. "Okay, off I go to the basement. I only have two more bottles left, and then I have some paperwork, and I'm out of your hair."

Cary flashed one of the glamorous fake smiles Isaac didn't like. Marigold didn't seem to mind, though, because she smiled right back at him.

"That's great, dear. Do you need Isaac?"

"I don't if you have something you need him to do today."

"Yes. We're getting ready for the harvest, and I'd really like for him to take part in that. It's important for him to see the preparations."

"THAT'S FINE." Cary told himself he wasn't disappointed, that it was fine if he was down there for only an hour or so on his own. But he'd miss Isaac's skin and his kisses and the way he smiled when Cary said something to him. He'd miss... Isaac.

You're such an idiot. This kid is a thief. He's screwing Marigold over as badly as you are, if not worse. Get away from him.

Too bad Cary's body didn't seem to care much. It only wanted to be nearer. Even with what he knew, Isaac still felt good to him, still felt right. He supposed he didn't mind a thief so much, and Marigold could probably spare the few things that had disappeared, but still, Isaac didn't have much of a future with her if she found out it was him. He wasn't making the best choices, and they weren't just bad for him.

Cary waved once more at the group in the kitchen and went for the wine cellar stairs. It cooled considerably as he walked down to the cellar.

The wine cellar had started to feel like home in a weird way. Maybe not so weird. He'd spent so much time in the damn place the past few days, trying to work his magic on Isaac and make his story credible. Trying to avoid letting Isaac get to him while he was at it. The hard part was about to start, though. He had to get these last bottles cataloged so he could show Marigold his work and make it all look shipshape before he started throwing doubts on a few bottles. Then the falsified authentication, the smear campaign on the sisters, and the offer.

He could deal with it. He could do it.

Cary started in the big locked section that held Marigold's most prized collector's items. Cary had spent hours in there the previous day, marveling over how much pure worth there was. He had only a little bit left to do. Two more bottles to catalog, photograph, and check, and then he was going to do one more overall sweep and he was done. Done. It felt good. Even though it wasn't really his job, he felt like he was doing it, accomplishing something. He was glad to be finished, though. He hadn't done this much paperwork since college.

While the cellar had started to feel homey, he kinda missed daylight and was more than ready to experience some of it again. He didn't want to turn into Lestat down there, after all. He finished with the pictures and the details on the two bottles. Made sure to match them up with their old assessment papers, and went about his overview. Everything was great until he ran across an empty spot.

Wait. There wasn't an empty spot there before.

The wines in this collection were moved if one was sold or used for some reason. As far as he knew, none of them had been used, and still the Château Pétrus was missing. Bottle number 65. He'd cataloged it the other day, taken a picture. Everything had been fine. It simply wasn't there. Just a gaping space where, the last time he'd been down that row, a bottle of wine had been. He thought it might have been about three days. Cary hadn't been down that row since the beginning of his work. He couldn't be certain how long the bottle had been missing. He just knew he was screwed.

He rushed through the rest of his overview, went back and checked the bottles around the missing spot, checked in other areas, made sure nobody had placed it in the wrong slot, and when he was sure the bottle wasn't in the cellar, he grabbed his things and headed up the stairs to look for Marigold.

Fuck. Fuck, fuck, fuck. Isaac, how could you?

He didn't want to blame him, but what were his choices? Bitchy Kitty had been down there the day before with his planted customer, but she'd never been alone. As far as he knew, she also didn't have permanent access to a key. Isaac knew exactly where Cary kept the copy he'd been lent for the audit and could've easily gotten to it while Cary was asleep. Shit. Unless he could prove Kitty had been down there tampering with the wines, he had to admit to himself that it had been Isaac. Marigold's lock-and-key security system sure as hell didn't include anything as high-tech as a surveillance camera. Cary ground his nails into the fleshy palm of his hand.

He found Marigold digging through the couch cushions with her housekeeper.

"Still no luck on the necklace?" Cary asked.

She popped her head up and looked at Cary. Poor thing seemed so annoyed. "None at all. I have no idea where it could be."

He felt a twinge. He knew exactly where Marigold's necklace was. It had been hocked days ago in San Francisco through their mutual friend Sandro. How the hell was Isaac managing to do it?

"Well, I might have some more bad news for you."

"What is it?" she asked.

"There's a bottle missing from the cellar. The 1946 Château Pétrus."

"I thought you only had a few left. How could one of them be missing?" Marigold asked sharply.

"I was just coming up here to make sure you hadn't decided to trade it, or use it."

"No. Of course not. I haven't touched anything from the collection. Just the wines from the other half of the cellar that we drink on a regular basis. It wouldn't make sense to disrupt the collection in the middle of your assessment even if I did want to do something with one of the bottles."

"That's what I thought. I looked all over the place, Mrs. Shelley. Unless I missed something very obvious, the bottle isn't down there. Isaac was with me when I cataloged it the first time. He can verify." Cary also had a sinking feeling he could probably tell her where he'd sold it too. He needed to talk to Jules.

"That's really odd. First my necklace, now this wine bottle. The house seems to have a poltergeist." She gave him an ironic smile. Cary tried to smile with her, but it was hard around growing fury.

It wasn't just the necklace and the bottle, though. It was a silver serving platter and earrings and a few other items as well. It was probably only a matter of time before Marigold noticed the rest of what was missing. He obviously couldn't tell Marigold what he knew, not without telling her why he knew as well, but he needed to talk to Jules, and then he needed to deal with Isaac. Of course Isaac had to be gone all day. Why would it be any different? The lack of Isaac left him with nothing to do but fake paperwork. It was time to see his girl face to face.

"Hey, I'm going to take a trip into town if you don't mind. I've been craving a Starbucks and some frozen yogurt. Do you want anything while I'm out? I'll look into the bottle again later before I start my paperwork. I don't want there to be any inconsistencies."

He also didn't want her to think it was him. At least he had the alibi of being with Isaac most of the time he'd been down there and clearly empty hands this time. He was mad, though. He'd be the first suspect, and he didn't want this shit to derail him.

"No, I think I'm fine, dear. Don't forget about dinner." Marigold smiled at him like she always had. She didn't seem suspicious, which again surprised him. She'd brought this stranger into her house and treated him like a friend, left him mostly alone with her priceless wine collection, and then didn't even act suspicious when a rather expensive bottle went missing. None of Marigold's actions made a lot of sense. Cary bit his lip for a minute before he remembered he was supposed to answer her.

"Oh, I won't miss dinner. I have a ton of work to do this afternoon, so I'll be back in an hour or two."

Marigold nodded. "Then I'm back to my necklace search. I'll add a bottle of Château Pétrus to that while I'm at it. Maybe that's hiding behind the couch cushions as well."

Cary wondered if he was hallucinating the slight look of suspicion in Marigold's eyes on that last answer or if it was really there. Cary sighed inwardly. If Isaac ruined this job for him, he was gonna kill the damn kid, hot in bed or not. Dead. End of story.

He left in his car and drove toward town, making sure he wasn't followed. There was no reason for him to be followed, but who knew what sources his mark had at her disposal and Cary wasn't in the habit of trusting people. It had kept him alive and mostly out of trouble for years. He stopped at a Starbucks, partly because Jules loved it, and also because he really liked to stick to as much of the truth as he could when he was running a job. After a short and frustrating encounter with a barista, who'd dubbed him "Carrie" according to his cup, he was on the road again.

He'd done a few laps, paranoid as usual, but was clear when he pulled into a spot at the hotel far from street view. He got out, balancing the teetering Starbucks cups and bags, and slid into the door of the hotel as unobtrusively as possible. He went into the elevator, riding it up to the floor where he shared a room with Jules. She was there, typing away at her phone, when he walked in.

She jumped. "Fuck, boss. You scared the hell out of me."

"Sorry, babe. Listen. I need to talk to you. A bottle of wine is missing from the special collection that was there the day I started my audit. I'm guessing it's our little sticky fingers, but this isn't going to look good for me, is it?"

Jules sighed. "I told you to shut that down. Why didn't you do it the first time? This is the kind of shit that happens when you don't listen to me."

"I haven't had the opportunity to shut the thief down yet. I meant to, but it just hasn't happened."

"I don't like this job, Cary. We need to pull out of there, and we need to do it now."

Cary's heart pounded at the thought of leaving. He wanted that damn wine. That was why he needed to stay. The wine. It had nothing to do with wanting to save Isaac from himself. "I'll take care of it. I just need to find that damn bottle and get it back. Can you see where it got fenced?"

Jules nodded. "I can try at least. I didn't see it coming through Sandro's records this morning, but another fence could've easily taken it. He's the easiest for me to watch, but there are dozens of others."

"Does Sandro know you have access to everything he does?"

Jules game him her typical look. "What do you think?"

Why did he even ask? "Point taken. Anyway, the thief probably wouldn't always go with the same fence."

"Can't you just say Isaac? We all know it's him as much as you might like it not to be."

"I don't care—"

"Try that on someone who will believe it. You care about people, Cary Talbot. Even when you sometimes shouldn't. Now. Let's all admit Isaac's the thief. Out loud."

Cary really hated that thought. "Fine. Isaac. Isaac might not always use the same fence when he sells things. Happy?"

"Always." She smirked. Cary shoved her. "Let me get to work on finding that fence who has the wine. Why don't you just keep things moving on your end? We'll need to have everyone set up to believe our story and sell you the wines. You don't have time to hunt down some low-level middle man."

"Yeah. I know."

Cary felt sick to his stomach about the whole thing. Maybe Jules was right, and he needed to get the hell out before things got any more complicated. Although he didn't know how, at this point, to get out. He was in it hard, and he'd been there so long there was no way he could melt into the background and disappear without causing a huge wave. And waves were the kinds of things that got people on those alphabet agency lists he was always trying to avoid. He didn't want any of those people after him. He didn't want anyone after him. He also didn't like the idea of Isaac hocking his grandmother's goods to low-level fences. He didn't even get why the hell he'd do it.

Cary shook it off and went out on their minuscule balcony to talk to their favorite go-to guy for fake documents, Steve. He was fantastic with wines, jewels, anything that needed to be "authenticated." Or, as in this case, not-thenticated. He was the best in the business.

"Hey, Steve. You okay to be on call the next few days?" he said as soon as Steve picked up.

"Yeah. I got a job out in Santa Fe, some forged Navajo relics need to be certificated for sale. I've gotta leave for there by next weekend, but until then I'm your guy."

"Jesus. If this isn't done by next weekend, I'm fucked."

"Yeah. Then we're good. You in Napa?"

"Close enough. Just outside of Sonoma."

"That whole area is all the same to me. Like a big old grape leaf."

Cary felt that way too. Well, he had a few days ago. But in his hotel room, nice and air-conditioned and away from everyone's curious eyes, he found himself missing the damn place.

Jesus Christ, I've only been gone an hour. Not even that.

He hung up with Steve after they'd set up everything, which wasn't much, honestly. Steve was great at his job, and that was one of the things Cary loved about working with him. Cary came back into the room to the tail end of Jules dealing with someone who hopefully was the fence who had their wine.

"He wants a fucking arm, leg, and horse for this bottle of wine. Seven Gs, can you believe it?"

"That's actually low for that bottle if I remember the paperwork correctly. Knowing Marigold's collection, it could've been a hell of a lot worse. Did we get confirmation?"

"Black hair, pale skin, big blue doe eyes, looks like a freaking kid."

That was Isaac. Shit. Every time he thought there wasn't a single damn way Isaac could've done it, he was proven wrong. This time by an eyewitness. Isaac had been there. Isaac sold the wine. He must've slipped out sometime early in the morning. Cary had woken up alone. He felt like he was going to puke.

"What are you going to do, boss?"

"I'm going to deal with it. I wasn't going to touch the jewelry, but this is going to come back and bite me in the goddamn ass if I don't do something. So I guess I'm going to have a talk with our enterprising young thief."

"I'm sorry. I know you liked him."

"Since when does someone being a thief mean I can't like them anymore?" Cary smirked. "Some of my best friends have been criminals." He punched Jules lightly on the shoulder. "Still are."

"Back at ya."

"But he's going to have to stay out of my way. And *that* we're going to need to discuss. Now I'm going to get to drive to—"

"Oakland."

Fuck. Oakland. "I'm going to drive to Oakland and buy back that fucking wine so I don't get my ass sent to jail for thieving."

"You're really going for the long game on this one. I've never seen you shell out that much for a mark."

"This one is different. I don't even know why anymore. Maybe it's just so I can say I did it. Other than that, I wasted all this time playing around in a wine cellar for nothing and will probably get in trouble to boot. I have a fun drive ahead of me, and I have to be back soon. I've gotta go."

"Sorry, man. I'd do it but—"

"No. I need to get the wine back onto the property and into the cellar somehow. Then I can bring it up from there and everything will be A-OK. They're probably still going to look at me like I'm a moron but still. At least I won't be a thief. Yet."

Jules snickered and pushed Cary. "Go. Get the hell out. You have things to do, and you're wasting my afternoon."

"You love me." Cary made exaggerated kissy faces at Jules. She gave him another shove.

"So much."

Nothing like annoying Jules to make a crappy day better. "You miss having me around every day."

"Like I miss getting tetanus shots in my eyeballs."

"You wound me. It hurts."

Jules surprised Cary by giving him a sweet kiss on the cheek. "Quit being a smartass and get to work."

"We're not done with this conversation."

"There is no conversation."

Cary walked to the elevator laughing. Jules and he, well, they were special. And he didn't mean Hallmark special, he meant sometimes it was amazing they didn't kill each other. Lovingly, of course.

He hopped into his car after a short elevator ride and a watchful jaunt through the lobby, and drove south toward Oakland and one very expensive bottle of wine.

The fences didn't do things the way they used to. What had been dirty envelopes of cash back in the day was now done with wire transfers to and from untraceable accounts that probably had their origins somewhere in the Caymans. It was complicated and sticky, way too high-tech for his taste, and left an unfortunate trail that they probably thought was invisible but people like Jules could easily decipher. Sometimes Cary wondered what had been wrong with the old way of doing things.

Cary had done his share of trades with fences, had many more in the future, but they always made him kinda antsy. He pulled up to the location about an hour later and looked around. He'd never dealt with this one before, and there was nothing more unsettling than a new fence. They could kill you as easily as give you the merchandise once you transferred the funds. This wasn't his favorite part of the job.

It wasn't bad, though. Turned out he'd done all that stressing the whole drive down for no reason. He dealt with the money transfer, confirmed with the fence that it was in fact Isaac who'd sold him the wine—the guy recognized a picture of him and said he was sure—and then hopped in his car with the wine and a lot less money, and got on the highway back into wine country.

It was late when Cary got back to Falling River. He was barely going to have a chance to relax for a minute before it was time to get ready for dinner. He'd just collapsed onto his bed when the door to the guesthouse slid open. There was Isaac, standing there all cute and adorable. He didn't look like anything Cary would've called a thief. Still. Knowing he'd done it, that he'd managed to steal the wine and fence it, Cary couldn't see it. He didn't want to make generalizations, but there was a look to people who did what he and Jules did. A loss of innocence or a tarnish. After all his years on the street, Isaac didn't have it.

Cary was confused, and he was mad. Mad that he'd had to waste his own money, mad that he'd barely managed to slip down to the wine cellar and stick it in the wrong place before Kitty found him. He was just mad. And it wasn't even that Isaac was working directly against him. Well, except the wine. Even a moron of a thief would know that was going to make Cary, the insurance guy who'd been down in the wines all week, look like he'd taken it.

Cary didn't want to deal with it. He also didn't want to deal with getting changed and going down to dinner, but he had to.

"Hey, Isaac."

"Long day?" Isaac looked kind of tired too. Like maybe someone who'd gotten up in the morning, driven all the way to Oakland, and made it back in time to do a whole day out on the vineyard. Yeah. That kind of tired. Cary winced when he sat up.

"Yeah. Long day," he lied. Well, it wasn't exactly a lie, but he gestured to his stacks of paperwork and made it seem like that was the reason. Cary didn't know what he was going to do when he got a look at Isaac's face later. When he announced he'd taken another look around in the cellar and found the bottle in the wrong place. Isaac was probably going to freak. Cary didn't blame him. Anyone would freak out if something showed back up when they were completely sure they'd stolen it.

"Here," Isaac said, reaching out to rub his shoulder. "Why don't I grab some dinner clothes and you take a quick shower. I bet you're hot. You were in the car driving around for a while too, weren't you?"

"Marigold really doesn't keep any details to herself, does she?"

"Was it a secret?" Isaac looked hurt for a moment.

"Of course not, but it wasn't exactly supposed to be public either. I don't need the whole staff knowing where I am at all times."

"Hey," Isaac said gently. "It was just me, and it was only because I asked when I came in at lunch. I wanted to see you." He leaned over and brushed a kiss across Cary's lips. "You really are tired, aren't you? You wanna skip dinner?"

Yes. But he was really hungry too. "No. I'll go hop in the shower. Pick me out something light. I'm boiling in here."

He wanted to say something to Isaac, like maybe "Why the fuck are you fucking me over?" But he didn't. They had to be in the big house in ten minutes. Fifteen, if they were cutting it really close. He didn't have time for that talk. Not yet. He didn't know if he wanted to get into it after dinner either. He was exhausted. He only wanted to go to bed. Cary could see Jules in his head, rolling her eyes and *tsking* at him for being a fucking chicken. He wasn't a chicken. He was going to do it. He just wanted to put it off for one more night, that's all.

"Hey, you okay with that peach button-up?" Isaac called from the main room. He sounded cheery and content. He had no idea what was coming his way.

"Sure," Cary muttered. Honestly, he didn't care as long as it covered his chest and wasn't too hot.

Dinner was long, but filling and good. The chef had made enchiladas, which had always been one of Cary's favorites. They were filled with tons of local ingredients and smothered with cheese and sauce. Cary managed to scarf down three of them and a side of seasoned rice. It was quite a feat, seeing as Cary nearly nodded off once or twice. He wanted nothing more than to return to his room with a full belly and close his eyes, but he couldn't escape without making his big announcement. He waited until the main course was cleared and dessert was on the way.

"Oh, I have good news," he said to Marigold, his eye halfway on Isaac at the same time.

"That's fantastic, dear. What is it?"

"I found the Pétrus. It was really just a mistake. I didn't check the last row of empty racks. I have no idea how it got over there." Cary smiled sheepishly. "Maybe I left it on a shelf when I was organizing and someone didn't want to put it in the wrong spot?"

Isaac beamed. Not the reaction Cary was expecting. Wow. Not the reaction he was expecting at all. Isaac looked genuinely thrilled to have the wine back in Marigold's possession.

"That's great. I know it would be such a pain trying to track one of those bottles down again. Aren't some of them impossible to replace?" he asked Cary, eyes wide.

Jesus Christ, he's good. There wasn't a drop of panic in Isaac's eyes. His facial muscles were relaxed, no signs of distress, only pure happiness that Cary had found his grandmother's dumb wine. Seriously. A master. If he wasn't so pissed at the shit for nearly ruining his con, he'd hire him on the spot.

"Yes, so disaster averted. You can cross the wine off your list of lost items."

"Still haven't found my necklace," Marigold grumbled.

Cary fought the instinct to track that necklace down to Sandro and buy it back. Jesus, at that rate, by the time he left, Marigold would owe him money, not the other way around. He did feel bad, though. It would suck to lose something that important.

By the time they got out to the guesthouse, all Cary wanted to do was sleep, curled in the navy blue duvet and Isaac's arms. Yes, he wanted to sleep in Isaac's arms. He also didn't want to examine that fact.

Cary didn't want to talk about the stealing. He just wanted to sleep. And the fact that he got to fall asleep next to Isaac was pretty nice. He stripped down to his boxers and flopped on the bed.

"You okay?" Isaac asked. He still hadn't broken about the wine bottle. Not even a little. It looked like it had totally slipped his mind. Cary had no idea how he'd managed to stay so calm.

"Yeah. Just really, really exhausted."

"Here, pick your feet up." Isaac dragged the covers from underneath his legs and draped them over Cary's midsection. "Close your eyes. I want to wash my face off and stuff, and I'll be in. I'm pretty tired too. Long day in the sun."

"You got up really early, didn't you? You were gone by seven."

Isaac chuckled from the bathroom. "I left way before that. Walk of shamed it back to my room and passed out for another hour or two. Of course I ran into my grandmother on the way there so I didn't exactly not get noticed sneaking out of your room."

"You went back to sleep?"

"Yeah." Isaac giggled again. "What else was I going to do at five in the morning? Write a few sonnets? I don't know why I bothered. Marigold totally doesn't care. I think she likes that we're into each other."

Cary couldn't put it together. Isaac hadn't been in Oakland all morning unless he was an amazing liar. He'd been in bed? But the guy had seen him. Sure, the description was kind of vague, but what other dark haired, blue-eyed pale kids would be walking around with a very rare bottle of wine? And he'd recognized the picture. Cary couldn't forget that part. The whole thing made his head hurt. He didn't want to think about it. No news there. Mostly, he wanted to curl up and close his eyes. So he did. He barely noticed when Isaac got into bed behind him and wrapped his arms around Cary's waist.

"Night, Cary," he whispered into his neck.

Cary patted tiredly at Isaac's hand. "Night," he muttered.

Cary woke in the middle of the night, Isaac's warm body against his, his arms still wrapped loosely around Cary's waist. He didn't know what to think about Isaac, about the stealing, about anything, but there was one thing he could count on.

He hadn't ever wanted anyone as much as he wanted Isaac. The constant need thrumming beneath his skin was nearly impossible to control and nothing like he'd ever felt, even when he'd been a teenager and constantly horny. He only wanted it more after he'd been inside Isaac, had Isaac touching every part of him. He'd been satisfied for the night, but instead of getting bored and wanting something new, like he usually did, he wanted Isaac again. In the same ways, in different ways. Just Isaac. Isaac mumbled and ruffled Cary's hair.

"Can't sleep?"

"Just woke up. I guess I was having a bad dream."

"Mm. C'mere." Isaac rolled Cary over and pulled him into a kiss.

"Sorry. Didn't mean to wake you up," Cary mumbled into the kiss. But he didn't really mind if he got kisses.

"Don't be sorry." Isaac slid his hands up and down Cary's back like he always did. It seemed like he couldn't get enough of Cary's skin. Cary knew the feeling.

"Take these off," Isaac murmured. He pulled at Cary's boxer briefs until Cary lifted his hips and shimmied them down and off. Isaac made quick work of his own bottoms and draped his leg over Cary's hip.

"What are you doing?" Cary asked quietly. He nipped at Isaac's neck and shivered when Isaac drew a finger down and tested his hole.

"I want in here," Isaac murmured. "I thought about it all day yesterday."

"Yeah?"

"You feel amazing. I want to feel it again."

Cary flipped over and reached into his nightstand. He wasn't going to say no to more Isaac. More skin and sweat and his pretty, thick cock. He passed the lube to Isaac, who made quick work of slicking up his fingers.

"Like this," Isaac said. "I want to fuck you like this."

He'd been so shy that first night, like he wasn't quite sure what to do. Cary barely knew how to handle this Isaac, the one who was sexy and sure of himself. And if he kept talking like that, well Cary wasn't going to have much of a chance to handle him at all. He'd lose it before they even got started.

"Yes. I want that."

Isaac sucked on Cary's neck and slowly pushed his fingers in. "You like when I fuck you like this?" Cary choked. Where was this coming from? He couldn't concentrate on anything but the way Isaac's fingers felt inside him, slim and strong, curling to hit him in all the right places. Cary grabbed for Isaac's other hand, the one that was on the pillow holding him steady.

"You like it?" Isaac repeated.

"Y-yeah. I like it."

"You want more?" He crooked his fingers perfectly and pressed hard.

Cary let out a long groan. "Fuck. Yes. I want more."

"You want me?"

"What's got, *fuck*, what's got into you?" Cary bit at his bicep.

Isaac let out a breathless moan. "I don't even know. I just want you. Constantly."

"Yes. Now."

Cary waited the long seconds it took Isaac to prepare. Then he was back, thick and slick, pushing against Cary's entrance. He came in on a groan, slow and steady and hot. Isaac pulled Cary's leg up to sling over his hip, opening him up.

"Move," Cary said. "Please."

Isaac moved, slowly at first, questioning, until he found the exact right spot. Cary burst into shivers.

"There?" Isaac whispered against his neck.

"Yes, Jesus. There."

He picked up his pace again, hand curled around Cary's hip, angled just right, whispering hot, dirty things into Cary's ear about how much he wanted this, and how warm and tight and good it felt. He rubbed against Cary's prostate, hitting it every damn time, until

Cary was a shuddering, sweaty mess, teetering on the edge but unable to fall.

"You think you can come from just my cock in you?" Isaac asked.

Cary hauled in a breath and clenched his jaw. He was so fucking close, just from Isaac's slow, deep strokes, the way their skin felt, the words whispered in his ear.

"Touch me, please." Cary hadn't ever been a beggar in bed, but he was desperate.

"Okay." Isaac slid his hand down Cary's hip and wrapped it around his straining cock. There it was. It only took a few short strokes, and he was there, blacked out and coming harder than he'd ever come before.

CHAPTER 8

ISAAC HAD been out with Marigold all morning, but he couldn't wait to get back to the house. He knew Cary had been cooped up all morning with paperwork and probably needed to get out and do something in the sun for a few hours. Nothing wrong with a little break, right? It had been absolute torture to follow Marigold around all morning to the shops, to lunch with one of her friends, but they'd also gone to the lawyers for another meeting. One step closer to being Isaac Shelley officially. One step closer to the trust fund. Isaac was annoyed at himself at how easily he'd gotten distracted from his goal thinking about how much he wanted Cary. But he wasn't going to let it happen anymore after this evening.

He thought maybe he could get Cary into the pool, play a few games, take a nap with him on one of the huge cushy poolside chairs that were big enough for two, spooned and warmed from the sun. Then maybe Cary could spend an hour or so on work before dinner. It seemed like a good plan to Isaac. Or they could stay inside. You know, with no clothes on. That would be a good plan too. He bounded over to the guesthouse as soon as he was sure Marigold was happy in her chair with a cup of iced tea, a muffin, and her book.

Cary wasn't working when he got in. He was perched on the edge of the bed. He looked tense. Isaac didn't like tense Cary.

"Hi," he said and sank down next to Cary. He wanted to wrap himself all around him like he usually did, like he had the night before. Isaac didn't have much willpower when it came to saying no to Cary. Or to himself where Cary was involved.

"Hi." Cary's voice was tight. Clipped.

"What's wrong?" Isaac asked. He didn't get why Cary was acting so strange. Things had been great between them that morning when he'd left with Marigold after breakfast. He thought, at least. "You're acting weird. I don't get it. What happened between this morning and now?"

"I'm acting weird?" Cary said. His voice was chilly. Isaac hated it.

"Yeah. You're acting super weird. Are you still on edge about that bottle of wine? I mean, you just put it in the wrong place, right? Things are fine now, or is there something wrong with your paperwork? Do you have to test any of the bottles for being fakes?" He kept babbling because he felt uncomfortable. Cary never made him uncomfortable but he was. And the way Isaac always dealt with that was questions. Lots of them. He made himself shut up.

"Yes, I actually am going to want to run a few tests just to be sure on some of them. Particularly… well, really it's not about that."

"What is it about, then?" Isaac shifted so he could look Cary right in the eye. That was if Cary would look at him.

"You."

"Me?" Isaac's stomach swooped hard. He hadn't done anything, had he? Was this Cary telling him he was bored? That the job was almost done and he was leaving and Isaac shouldn't be a total child about the fact that they were probably done?

Fuck.

Really, you moron. It's only been a few days. Still, it already hurt, and Cary hadn't even said it yet.

"Is this where you say that you're packing up to go soon and I shouldn't expect much?"

"No, this is where I tell you to quit getting in my way."

Well, that wasn't quite what he expected. "Getting in your way? What are you talking about?"

Cary slid a sheet of paper toward him. It was a printout of a receipt or something with a signature scrawled on it. It looked like the signature said Isaac Shelley, but it sure as hell wasn't his. Isaac was confused. More than confused, but he was trying not to act like it. "What's this?"

"This is the sheet from the lowlife fence who bought that bottle of missing wine. Also, from Marigold's missing necklace." Another sheet. "And the missing silver tray she hasn't even noticed is gone yet." A third. "I had to drive all the way into Oakland yesterday to get that damn bottle back or else your lovely step-grandmother would've thought I'd taken it and probably had me arrested. I paid a lot more money than I have in my budget for this job, and I don't want to do it again. I'd also really like to not get arrested, so I'd appreciate if you'd knock it the fuck off with the sticky fingers routine until I'm done and out of here."

"Wait. You think I stole these things?" Not that he'd never stolen anything before, but he'd never do that to Marigold. Why would he steal her necklace or wine when that would ruin everything he'd worked for? Isaac would have to be an idiot. And he couldn't imagine how Cary would believe he'd do something like that.

"Obviously. The signatures point pretty strongly in your direction. Listen, I don't care if you do it after I'm done here, but I don't want any more of this. You're messing up my job, kid. You're complicating things, and I can't have that."

Isaac cocked his head to the side. "Wait a second. You honestly think I've been stealing things from Marigold? *Honestly?*"

"Didn't I just say that? What else am I supposed to think?"

Isaac scoffed to cover up the unreasonable hurt that sliced him. He got it. The evidence was pretty damning. Still. "Maybe you could've tried asking?"

Cary snorted. "Yes. Let me see how that would've gone. Isaac, are you stealing from your grandmother?"

Something in Cary's tone irritated the hell out of Isaac. "And my answer would've been 'No, you giant asshole.' That would ruin all the plans I have for getting her to sign my trust fund over to—shit."

Isaac had never been good at controlling his temper. Or his mouth. It was one of the things Roman had been working on with him. Not very good at all.

"Trust fund. Is that what this is about?" Cary cocked his head to the side.

In that moment, something clicked. Maybe it was the conversation, the small moments adding up to the second when Isaac realized exactly where he'd seen Cary before. His hair was a lot lighter, he was an insurance auditor instead of a gemologist, but he was the same damn grifter who'd screwed Roman out of three huge emeralds in New York nearly two years ago. *I knew I knew him. Jesus.*

"You asshole!" Isaac pushed him.

"What the fuck?"

From Cary's point of view that had probably seemed a little crazy, but Isaac had no problem explaining himself. None at all.

"I know you. You never saw me, but I saw you for damn sure."

"What the hell are you talking about? You've never met me before."

Isaac wished that was true. "I haven't met you, but an associate of mine has. New York City, about two years ago. There were a few very large and very rare emeralds that you declared fake just in time to steal them out from underneath Roman's nose. I know you. You're not even playing a different game. Priceless wine and insurance auditor isn't really all that different than priceless emeralds and gemologist, is it? Not when you're doing the same thing. Jesus Christ, how could I have been so dumb?"

"You work for Roman?" Cary looked shell-shocked. "You're... you.... Damn."

"Yes, I work for Roman. At least I did until he had to take off out of the country. That guy was the closest thing I ever had to a family. So thanks for that."

"I didn't do anything to him."

Isaac shrugged. He was beyond the point of wondering how Cary could believe that of him and into the territory of angry as hell. "Maybe if he'd had those emeralds still he would've been able to buy some favors and stick around." Isaac knew he wasn't being rational but it wasn't easy. Everything hurt. His chest, his belly. He felt sick.

"So let me get all of this straight. You're here for the trust fund. Isaac Shelley's trust fund."

"Yes." Short answer, at least.

"And you're not Isaac Shelley?"

Isaac snorted. "I highly fucking doubt it."

"And I'm here for the Nine Sisters. Nothing else."

"Good to know." *Especially good to know you're not here for me. Just in case I had any delusions there was really something going on here.*

"And I'm not an insurance auditor."

"Guess that's pretty much out the window, Cary. If that's even your name."

"It is. Most of the time at least. Are you working alone?"

"Yes. Are you?"

"No."

"Then how am I supposed to know that your little helper didn't steal the goods and act like I did it?"

"First of all because some of them were gone before we even decided to come here. Second, why would she screw me over like that? Stealing that wine made me look very suspicious."

"Is it Kitty? Is she your helper?" The thought of that just about made Isaac want to puke.

Cary choked. "*No.* Of course not. You've never seen my associate. Nobody here has."

Isaac wanted to lash out somehow. He was pissed, and he felt like there was nothing he could do. Except. "What if I told Marigold what you were doing?"

"What if I told her what you were doing?" Cary shrugged. "You're in just as much trouble as I am. Only, I wasn't here when the first few items were hocked, was I? I think that means the finger won't be pointing at me."

"I'm her grandson, though."

"Not if I tell her you're a con artist."

Isaac stood there silently for a moment. "And would tattling on me be worth it? It would just make you look guilty too. Since you know and all."

Cary sighed. "I can't fucking believe this. What a mess."

"What, that we're both in this for money?" Isaac shrugged. He was trying to keep his cool, but he was as angry as Cary was. Far angrier, probably. There went the afternoon in the pool and snuggling on the damn chair. There went a lot of things, including his pride. Hopefully his freedom didn't vacate the premises right along with it.

"No, I can't believe that I couldn't fucking tell you were. I didn't even want to believe you were stealing her stuff. The fact that you're one of us…. How could I not *tell*?"

"I wasn't stealing her stuff. I haven't taken a damn thing. Why would I steal a necklace or a bottle of wine when I could have Isaac Shelley's trust fund?"

"So… shit." Cary shook his head slowly.

"What?"

"There's someone else here."

Isaac shrugged. "Not my problem."

"Oh, it very much is your problem since they seem to be wanting to frame you."

Isaac sat down on Cary's bed. "The way I see it is, I can't tell if it's you. You screwed Roman. Why wouldn't you do the same thing to me as well? How do I know you didn't plan all this weeks before you got here just to get me out of your way?"

Cary looked frustrated. "Because I wouldn't have stolen a wine bottle. Do you not get how bad that makes me look? I didn't do this, and if you didn't either then at least one of us has a very big problem. I don't give a shit what you're after. You want the trust fund? Take it. Just stay the hell out of my way."

"Right. Like you stayed out of Roman's way?" Isaac's natural stubbornness wouldn't let that go.

"Forget Roman right now. You have bigger problems than me, kid." Cary stood and started pacing.

"Yeah. I do. Maybe if I get rid of you, I'll be able to deal with them."

"I wouldn't do that," Cary warned.

For the first time since they'd met, Cary looked dangerous. Like someone Isaac didn't instinctively trust. He remembered the night before, how close they'd felt, and not just their bodies, or at least Isaac hadn't thought so. Cary obviously hadn't felt things quite as keenly as hc had. He'd thought they were connected, that even if it was a fling, it had kind of meant something. It had to him. To Cary, he was a means to an end. And then a problem. Isaac tried not to let it hurt as much as it did.

"So... we're at a bit of an impasse, I think," he said. He tried to keep his voice from trembling.

"Yep. You screw me, I'll screw you right back."

"Likewise."

"Then we'll both be in trouble."

"Sounds about right," Isaac answered.

Cary sighed and clenched his jaw. "Good talk."

"Fuck off."

Isaac rose and walked to the door. He yanked it open, walked through, and pulled it shut as hard as he could. He only wished it was satisfying to slam sliding doors. Which obviously it wasn't.

He wanted to collapse into a pool chair and let himself be hurt for just a few seconds, but he didn't. He couldn't show weakness to this guy. Who knew how he'd use it? Isaac was on his own. He'd always been on his own, but for a few days, it hadn't seemed like it.

Quit being a moron. Get your head in the game.

He hadn't come to Falling River to fall for someone. He'd come to get more money than he'd ever seen before. It was time to remember that. Isaac stomped his way around the pool and paused to take a long, deep breath. *Play it cool.*

He didn't want Marigold to get wind of the argument. Obviously explaining wouldn't be the best idea, since the truth was a hell of a lot of messiness. And it was better to keep to as many truths as possible.

He can't prove you're a fake, he can't prove this was planned. As far as Marigold knows, she found you; as far as she knows, you don't know who the hell you are. That's completely true. Cary can't prove you're a con. He can't do anything to you. It's your word against his.

He had to keep that in mind if he wasn't going to fall apart. It was Cary's word against his. And he was the one that Marigold thought was her family.

Of course, Isaac didn't know what Cary was capable of. He had help. He could do things from a distance. Isaac was in so much trouble. He was happy it was past dinner. He and Marigold had eaten while they were out and everyone else had had something while they were gone. He didn't want to look at Cary's smug face while he sat there and told Isaac he couldn't do anything to hurt him without fucking himself in the ass. It was fantastic. Good times. And he'd gone over there ready to kiss and hug and cuddle. Now he wanted to fucking punch something. He had to chill out and find a damn good plan B.

CHAPTER 9

ISAAC WANTED to hide in his room all day. The rest of the week. The rest of his life maybe? He kept playing the day before over and over in his head, and the only thing that came out of it was embarrassment. Deep, impossible-to-forget embarrassment. Over and over and over he went, trying to figure out when he should've known. When he should've realized what was going on.

How the hell could he not have known who Cary was? He'd spent months fuming over the way he'd conned those damn emeralds out from underneath Roman's nose. Roman was one of the best. He wasn't supposed to get out-conned. He guessed Cary was one of the best too. Probably why nobody had ever heard of him. Despite the romantic ideas about recognition and infamy, it really was a good thing to not be notorious. Cary, according to everyone Isaac had ever met, didn't exist. That didn't mean much in the whole scope of things, though. He was still at Falling River, he was still after Marigold's wine, and he could still screw the hell out of Isaac. In the getting-him-arrested kind of way, not the hot, sweaty, rolling around in bed way. Well, he could do that too.

No. You don't want that with him anymore.

He wished he didn't. As angry as Isaac was, he still felt Cary everywhere on him, tasted his kisses, heard the words Cary had whispered in his ear. His skin still ached to be touched like it had been that last night in the guesthouse. His bed felt sad and empty. It was pathetic.

Isaac dragged himself out his lonely, empty bed and into a punishingly hot shower. He couldn't believe it. Part of him had known. How could he ignore his instincts? Isaac fumed as he washed his hair and scrubbed his back and legs. He was safe for the moment, but still angry at himself for not being able to see it from the start and ignoring himself when he finally started to recognize that Cary wasn't what he seemed. *Always a good idea to push your instincts down because you don't want to be wrong about a hot guy.* It was the first time Isaac had learned the lesson. He vowed for it to be his last.

"You're such a fucking idiot."

He got out of the shower and dried off, toweling his legs and arms and scrubbing angrily at his hair. He dressed in a pair of the jeans Marigold had bought him, tailored and expensive. Definitely not from the mall. He shoved his feet into a soft pair of Converses and pulled on a Henley. It was an overcast day, the first one in weeks, and the heat of late summer chilled dramatically as soon as the sun disappeared.

He had some work to do with Mike today, he thought, and maybe he'd take Marigold out to lunch if she wasn't busy, keep her out and go shopping perhaps, tour some of the other vineyards in the area? He wanted to stay the hell away from Cary. And he wanted to keep Marigold away from Cary's considerable convincing skills. It wasn't exactly getting in the way of Cary's plan, per se. It was just taking his fake step-grandmother out to lunch. And shopping. And a vineyard tour. Maybe he'd been planning on spending the day that way anyway. Cary couldn't accuse him of trying to sabotage his plan if Isaac didn't do anything overt. Right?

Cary was going to convince her the Nine Sisters were fake, obviously, and then buy them for a really low price so the insurance company didn't "go after her for fraud," just like he'd done before. It took a lot of fast-talking and data manipulation. Isaac assumed Cary had the means. He also assumed the bottles weren't fakes and probably worth a hell of a lot of money if they had garnered the attention of someone like Cary. Isaac doubted he spent his time or effort on run-of-the-mill things.

It really was the same damn game he'd been playing in New York with the emeralds. Must be one that he's good at. Cary obviously hadn't expected to be found by someone who'd watched him play it before. What was he going to do, round up some dude to give them a fake appraisal? Make a website or two showing the bottles had been "found" before and shown to be only a rumor? Isaac at least could guess at all of his tricks. He wasn't going to make it easy for the asshole. He also wasn't going to go out of his way to get Cary in trouble. They had their deal. As stated quite clearly, ruining Cary's plans would only result in getting his own ass kicked out and probably arrested.

Good times.

He limped down the stairs to the kitchen, tired and sore after a full night of not sleeping at all. He'd tossed and turned and punched his pillow until his bedroom filled with faint but still irritating light. He'd been able to close his eyes then. Wasn't that the way it worked? But it was only for an hour or so. Nowhere near enough. It was going to be a long day. "Morning, sweetheart," Marigold said with a grin when he sat at the table.

He felt a surge of guilt when he thought about taking the trust from her. But he was more pissed at the thought of Cary getting all those wines. They had to be worth a fucking fortune, and they were hers. Isaac found himself wanting to protect Marigold—take out the asshole who was framing him for the thefts, yeah, but his first instinct was to protect her, not himself. He even wanted to protect Marigold from himself… and from everyone like him. Another part of him thought it might be best if he disappeared in the middle of the night and never came back. Isaac wished that would be easier.

"Morning, Grandmother."

He poured her juice, like they'd been in the habit of doing since only a week or so after he arrived at the vineyard. He served himself yogurt and fruit, and topped it with some of Gretchen's homemade granola. It was good; Gretchen was a fantastic cook, but it tasted like cardboard in his mouth. Everything probably would until he got used to the idea of how hard Cary could fuck him in every one of the very worst ways.

"How are you today?" She cocked her head in concern. It was odd how well Marigold had gotten to know him. She was amazing at reading him. Much better than Cary, apparently, but still she wasn't good enough to have figured him out. It was surprising actually. Isaac knew his fake step-grandma was a smart woman. How could she not know?

"I'm a little tired. Didn't sleep well last night."

She made a concerned face. "Is the mattress in the guesthouse not very good? I thought I had them change that out last summer after I had all those guests."

Isaac choked on his yogurt. She'd just announced it like it was no big deal. Shit. "It's fine," he mumbled.

Cary chose that exact moment to come ambling in with a folder for Marigold to look at and his travel coffee mug. "Morning, everyone," he muttered. He slid into a space right next to Isaac. Isaac wondered if he was hallucinating the way he seemed to crowd into Isaac's space. Isaac didn't want to scoot closer to Marigold and look like something was wrong. He also didn't want to give into his damn body and scoot closer to Cary. Fuck. How many more days until Cary finished what he was doing and got the hell out? Too many. Not enough.

"Morning, Cary," he answered. He hoped it sounded friendlier and more inviting, less... fraught than he thought it probably did. Fuck again.

"So, Marigold. I'm nearly done. I ended up getting all the bottles passed through inspection, but our department has some concerns about one of your collections, and they'd like to get an independent expert out here to look at it."

Here's his game. *It begins.* Isaac thought back and realized it had begun days ago. Probably when Cary had started being super sweet to him to get him on his side. Isaac so loved being played. He wanted to rip chunks out of the table. And maybe Cary's skin.

"That's fine," Marigold said. "I don't have any concerns with those bottles since they've been in the family for years, but if the company would like to get them authenticated then I'm not going to object."

Cary gestured at the folder in his possession. "I'll need to get you to sign this, then, if you don't mind. It'll allow the testing to go forward and release my company from damages if something were to happen to any of the bottles during testing."

"I'll need to have my lawyer look it over. Is there any way—" She thought for a moment. "Actually, Isaac, I was going to ask you to go into town today anyway and talk to Rose about the flower arrangements for the dinner tonight. Can you take the folder to the lawyer's office while you're there?"

Yet another of Marigold's famous summer dinner parties. It had been in the plans for weeks, but Isaac had forgotten it in the rush of finding Cary. He hated those kinds of events. It should be something he was really good at, charming Marigold's guests, working the room, and he supposed on the surface he was fairly good at it. But he still hated it. It was harder work than pretty much any other part of his job, and he'd been doing one event after another since he came into Marigold's life. He was the talk of the town, after all. California's wine country might be world famous, but it was still a collection of very, very small towns with small town attitudes and the gossip to match. He supposed he didn't have too many more of them to deal with. If nothing else, they'd be too busy during the harvest. And maybe by then, he'd have his trust fund and could hit the road.

"Yeah. I can do that. You have that checklist for Rose?"

"I do. It's in my handbag." She smiled slyly. "And why don't you take Cary with you? You two can get something delicious for lunch while you're out. Take your time."

Cary nodded. He *nodded*. That bastard. Isaac was about to kill him. That was until he remembered he didn't exactly want Cary alone with Marigold anyway. As much as he thought a nice long angry car ride between them would be torture, he still wanted to keep Cary away from his grandmother as much as possible.

But hell if he was buying lunch.

One far too short hour later, they were in Isaac's car on the way to downtown Sonoma. It wasn't far, but the drive was along windy back roads, and it typically took way longer than Isaac wanted to be stuck in a car alone with Cary, whom he wanted to punch. A lot.

"I can't believe you agreed to come with me," Isaac fumed.

Cary stared out the window at the picturesque rolling hills and fumed right back. Quietly, of course. He had on sunglasses and a T-shirt, and for once he looked relaxed and casual, not like he was there for business. Isaac was irritated by how hot it was.

"How else was I supposed to know you weren't going to do something to undermine me?" Cary grumbled.

"We had a deal. Besides, I'm doing errands for Marigold, not calling the FBI. Also, I'm now apparently taking you out to lunch. Thanks for that, by the way." Isaac rolled his eyes in the direction of the passenger seat. Not quite punching, but it made him feel a little bit better about the ache of hurt in his belly. He'd really fucking liked Cary. It sucked.

"You'll survive. It's just lunch. What's the plan, then, go to the lawyer and tell him what I'm doing while I wait in the car?"

"No. Because it's the same lawyer who has to draw up the papers for my trust. I don't know what you'll do if I burn you, but I highly doubt it'll be good." Isaac snorted. "Like I said."

"Isn't this nice? We've reached such an agreement." Cary settled against the seat.

"Fuck you."

"Listen, I don't know why you're so angry. You're here doing the same damn thing I am. Just getting a small piece of Marigold's huge pie that she can easily afford to give away."

"I'm pissed because you ruined things for Roman." *And me. I'm pissed because I was dumb enough to fall for you when you were only using me.*

"It wasn't anything personal. It was just a job. I doubt he took it personally."

"No, but I sure as hell am."

"Give it a few years, kid, and you won't see things so black and white. It's kind of cute really. That you want to stick up for him so much."

Way to make me feel like a baby. You sure as hell didn't think I was a few nights ago, did you? "He was the only family I had. I want to protect him."

Cary was quiet for a minute. "See, here's what I don't get. So you say you're after the trust fund, right?"

"Yeah." Isaac wondered how stupid it had been to tell him that.

"Well, to get the trust, Marigold has to legally sign papers saying you're Isaac Shelley. If she does that, well, then you're Isaac Shelley."

"I know."

"And you've grown up not knowing who you were, right? Or was that part of the story you fed her?"

"No, that's true. It's always better to tell the truth as much as you can."

Cary looked taken aback by that for a moment before he spoke again. "Then you can have a hell of a lot more than a trust fund. Why don't you?"

"It wouldn't be right."

"Do you want to be Isaac Shelley? Or are you one of those people who really can't live without the game?"

Isaac felt a rough twinge. Of course he wanted to stay. Who the hell wouldn't want to stay? Marigold was sweet, her property was beautiful. Isaac was happy. He just couldn't. Anyway. Why the hell was he talking to Cary? He was pissed at Cary.

"I don't know what I want." Isaac went all tight again, like he did every time he remembered Cary was using him. "And I'm sure as hell not talking to you about it. Just… just sit there."

"Sit. Silently. Fantastic."

CARY HOPED Isaac took the shortest route into town. A big part of him was not thrilled about the afternoon ahead of him with angry, junior Roman. Sexy, soft Isaac was fine. This? It was a mess.

He should've guessed it, though. Isaac had all the hallmarks of Roman's teaching. Cary had run into Isaac's mentor quite a few times in the ten years he had been operating. Roman was smooth, but he had a rough background. His charm came from his guileless face and the way he could convince anyone he was a good guy. There wasn't any of the charm Cary used to operate. It all seemed so genuine. That's probably why Isaac could see his brand of it from a far, far distance. Cary's game didn't come from convincing everyone he was a sweet, down-home guy. He was slick and sophisticated. Most of the time. He sure as hell seemed to have lost that knack at Falling River. Hopefully he found it soon.

They pulled into town a little later and drove down one of the main streets toward a charming little brick building with white shutters and flower boxes full of marigolds. He supposed that was super cute. Marigold's lawyer had marigolds. Cary nearly gagged. His old feelings about cute were flooding back into his system.

Isaac gave him another one of those pained, untrusting looks. "I'm going to drop this folder off. Don't move."

Cary rolled his eyes. "Yeah, I'm just going to drive off and leave you here. Without keys. Go deal with your stuff. You're fine."

He watched Isaac slide out of the low car and amble into the law office with Cary's fake papers for the lawyer to look over. Cary wished he hadn't watched quite as closely, but he remembered how Isaac's ass looked out of those jeans, when it was bare and up in the air and his for the taking. He was so pretty, with his pale skin and nicely rounded muscles. Cary still wanted to taste. It kinda sucked that that portion of the week's entertainment was over. He'd miss it. He hated to admit it, but he was going to miss Isaac when it was time for him to leave. He wished he and Jules could've left under better circumstances.

He also tried to pretend the thought of not seeing Isaac again after everything was over didn't hurt. Cary wasn't very good at pretending. Or having feelings.

A few minutes later, Isaac came out of the lawyer's office, polite smile fading, storm clouds settling back in. Time for the florist.

"Am I going to have to wait outside at the flower shop too?" Cary asked. He drummed on the dashboard.

Isaac glared at him. "No, you can come in if you want. I just need to go over the arrangements before tonight, not that Rose probably needs my help. She's known Marigold and her taste far longer than I have. I can't believe my grandmother is having people over. I know she means well, but I swear I've been paraded in front of half of California since I moved in."

Isaac had moments where he forgot how mad he was at Cary, when he could talk to him again. Cary saw it in his face. He needed someone to talk to too. Clearly, since Cary doubted he even realized he'd just called Marigold his grandmother without even thinking about it.

"Are you sure you want to just take the trust and run?" Cary asked.

"I already said I'm not talking about that with you. Just sit please. It's not very far from here. I really would rather we don't talk on the way."

"Onward we go, Miss Daisy."

"Wouldn't you be Miss Daisy?"

"I think I'm going to stay away from the flower names. They seem to be contagious around here, and I'm fine with my own."

Isaac scoffed. "If that even is your name."

"I already told you. It has been for so long, it might as well be. *Isaac.*"

"Touché."

The flower shop was picturesque, brightly painted, and filled wall-to-wall with refrigerators of flowers. Not surprising. The center section had a huge array of them, buckets tightly packed with stems, colorful and bursting with multicolored blooms.

"Rose?" Isaac called.

"Rose and Marigold?"

Isaac smiled. "I guess they've been friends for years."

"See what I meant about the flower names?"

"Yes, Miss Daisy." Isaac chuckled. Cary elbowed him.

A lady nearly Marigold's age shuffled out of the back room with a huge basket full of, well, roses. She looked as well-kept as Marigold did, expensive but casual. She smiled at Isaac.

"Hello, sweetheart. How are you today?"

Cary wondered why the flower lady knew Isaac so well.

"I'm good, Rose."

She sighed. "I wish so much that you remembered me. You were such a sweet little boy. You had so much fun when you were a boy clipping the flowers for me while your grandmother and I had tea. You're a wonderful man too. I'm excited to get to know you better."

Well, that was odd. Two people who knew junior Isaac and had total belief this Isaac was who he said he was. Cary wondered what it was that made him seem so familiar to them.

Isaac shook his head. "I wish I remembered too, but I don't. Years of my life are totally blank other than a shadow here or there, and I think they probably always will be. There's not much I can do about it."

Rose reached up and cupped Isaac's face. "It's okay, dear. Are you here to finalize the arrangements for tonight? Marigold said something about sending you over. I swear that woman hasn't learned the value of a telephone."

Isaac laughed. "Yes. Are you going to be there?"

She made a face. "Probably not. I'm not one for the big dinners. Your grandmother invited me, but I think I'll hold off until it's something more personal. I don't like crowds."

"I don't really like them either," Isaac said quietly.

Cary wondered how much he actually hated being paraded around. Was it a reaction to something that had happened, or was he nervous and waiting for someone to call foul on his game? Usually a grifter was at home in a crowd, but Isaac seemed to be telling the truth. Cary couldn't imagine trying to pull off what Isaac was doing. But it seemed like it had worked very well on the person that counted.

It was warmer when they got out of the florist shop, but overcast and cool compared to how it had been for the past few weeks. Cary watched Isaac push the sleeves of his Henley up and tried not to drool over the way the dark green looked against his fair skin. He'd gotten a bit more tanned the day when he was out with Mike in the vineyard, but he was still so pretty and pale. Especially underneath his clothes. Cary, as wary of Isaac as he was, wanted another taste. He missed it. He'd dreamed about it the night before, him and Isaac in bed kissing, Isaac on him naked. It was frustrating as hell to wake up alone and horny. Alone, he was used to. Horny hadn't happened since he was a sexually frustrated bisexual kid in a small Midwest town. He didn't want to experience it again.

"What do you want for lunch?" Isaac said.

"What's around here?" Cary asked. He was surprised Isaac's tone was cordial, seeing as how they'd been about to tear each other's throats out earlier.

"There are a few sit-down places, but they're going to be packed with tourists this time of year. I could take you to my favorite burrito joint. I used to go there at night when I got off work at the café. No tourists. Lots of cheese."

"Good?"

Isaac rolled his eyes. "No, I hated it. Yeah, they're great. It's super casual. Just a bunch of picnic tables and someone behind a counter making burritos you'll drool over."

"That sounds like my kinda place."

"Of course it does. You wouldn't be the kind of guy who could only eat in fancy restaurants."

Cary made a face. "What's that supposed to mean?" He knew somehow that Isaac was insulting him, but he didn't want to sit there and figure out how.

Isaac slid behind the wheel of his sleek—and probably very new—car and let Cary take the passenger seat again. Cary wouldn't have minded driving Isaac's pretty-mobile, but he didn't say anything about it. In fact, he stayed quiet the entire time they drove to the burrito place. Probably better not to talk and get Isaac pissed at him again. He was there to watch and make sure the kid didn't get him into any trouble. He wasn't there to cuddle and make friends.

Isaac's favorite burrito place was off the main drag of touristy, foofy cafés and restaurants owned by televisions chefs. It was more toward the highway in what actually looked like a residential neighborhood. Isaac pulled up to an unassuming building not much larger than a hut. It had probably once been some sort of drive-through. But they'd painted the building a bunch of bright colors, decorated the yard with Chinese lanterns and fabric bunting, and covered the picnic tables with cheerful cloth. It looked homey and perfect.

"What's good here?" Cary asked when they were standing in front of the counter looking at the extensive menu.

"You like fish burritos?"

"This is California, isn't it?" Cary asked.

Isaac let himself smile for once. "True, but you are from, you know... Oregon."

Cary chuckled a little. "I am. Try not to hold it against me. I'd love a fish burrito. Extra sauce if they have it. And a pineapple Jarritos." He pulled enough money out of his wallet for what he hoped were two meals and handed it to Isaac.

"Grab us a table. I'll order," Isaac said.

Cary found a table in the corner, with a bright pink cloth and a collection of garish silk flowers in a jar. It was cute and happy. It worked in an ironic sort of way.

Isaac came back with a basket of chips and a collection of dips: a little bowl of queso, liquidy green salsa, refried beans, and a fourth of pico de gallo. He also had two drinks.

It had been ages since Cary had chips and soda, but he wasn't going to complain. They dug into the food instead of talking much. Cary supposed they didn't have a lot to say to each other, other than vague threats mixed with the occasional friendly jab. It wasn't as if he was going to tell Isaac any of his trade secrets, and he highly doubted Isaac wanted to share anything with him. Especially since he seemed to hold a pretty hefty grudge against him for the business with Roman. Whenever he remembered to be angry, that was.

So instead, he ate chips. He had to agree they were amazing. Clearly not store bought, they were crispy and a tiny bit tender. Still warm, coated with a satisfying amount of salt and oil. He wanted to take the whole queso for himself and have a nice little pig-out. But then the burritos were placed in front of them, and they were huge, piled high with cheese and sauce, and squished on the plate next to sides of beans and rice.

"This is enormous. How did you ever deal with all of this?"

Isaac raised his eyebrows. "I'd eat it if I were you. Dinner parties usually consist of designer appetizers and small portions. It's not exactly homestyle cooking. I learned that the hard way. Let's just say I made my way out here for a midnight run the night after the first soiree."

"Thanks for the advice."

Cary took it. He dug into his burrito like he had the chips, and mouthful after mouthful disappeared from his plate and Isaac's as they both ate. He used chips to scoop up the beans and rice, and washed it down with gulps of pineapple soda. It was one of the best meals he'd had in days. Weeks even. He hoped his dress pants buttoned later. It wasn't guaranteed.

They'd just finished up and were about to throw their garbage in the provided can when Cary noticed someone watching him inquisitively.

Jules.

Apparently her stomach had led her here too. Shit.

"Why's that chick watching us?" Isaac said. Immediately he looked wary.

Jules hadn't gotten used to the old "pretend you don't know him and walk away" trick. She wasn't talking, but she was acting very awkward. Cary shrugged.

"She probably thinks you're hot? I don't know. Let's go unless you want to talk to her." Cary helped clear the papers up and placed their little plastic bins in the container provided for them. He ushered a worried-looking Isaac toward their car.

Jules whispered at him when he walked past. "I'm glad I ran into you. I've gotta talk to you tonight. Call me."

Her whispering skills weren't very good either. *Jesus, Jules. There's this thing called texting. Try it sometime.*

"Who the hell are you?" Isaac said. Jules looked surprised. Hell if Cary knew why. She'd said that about as loud as possible, so she couldn't have been shocked when Isaac reacted.

"I'm Jules."

Cary was seriously never sending her into the field. Ever. Zero skills.

"You his helper?"

Cary wanted her to lie, but she said "Yes" like it was no big deal. He thought he might strangle her if he ever got the chance.

Isaac glared at Jules. True to form, she glared right back. She might have championed him back when she thought he was a helpless innocent right off the street but clearly those feelings had changed rather quickly.

"Are you the one stealing shit in my name?"

"Of course not. Don't be stupid, kid."

Cary nearly laughed at her calling Isaac "kid" like he had at first. He was pretty sure they were the same age. Details.

She wasn't done talking. "Plus, we've got bigger problems now. I need to get back to the stuff but call me. There's a… new development in the job. I'd prefer not to talk about it here."

"Fantastic," Cary said. Developments were rarely good.

"A hell of a lot less than fantastic. Trust me, you're not going to like this."

That was pretty much what he'd expected.

Cary was tense the whole way back to Marigold's house. He didn't like whatever it was that Jules was implying. If it was worse than Isaac stealing things… what the hell was going to be worse than that? He didn't want to think about it. Isaac drove again and Cary stared out the window. The waves of pretty vines weren't so pretty any longer, not when he was sitting there waiting for Jules to drop a bomb.

"That didn't sound so good." Isaac sounded a little smug. Bastard.

"Yeah. I'll call her in the morning. Whatever it is can wait." So maybe he was putting his head in the sand, but he didn't have the energy to deal with something "worse" than everything else that was going on. If she told him, he'd have to do something. If he did something, well it never ended there, did it? Cary sighed.

"You sure? I mean, what if someone's after you? That wouldn't be good. What if someone called the feds?"

"Did you call the feds, you little shit?"

Had he thought Isaac cute a few minutes ago? No. No, he had not, damn it. If there was anything in the whole universe Cary didn't need, it was the FBI's white-collar crime bastards all over him. They were worse than the most persistent hunting dogs. They were impossible to shake once they got their claws in someone. Cary had remained unknown to them for many years. He'd like to keep it that way.

"No, I didn't call the fucking feds. We've been over this. I won't screw you, you won't screw me." He glared at the road with this stubborn, pissy look on his face.

"Then quit threatening me. That's annoying. Either do something or let me run my damn job in peace."

"I wasn't threatening you, just mentioning a possibility."

"That mention sounded awfully threatening. Just make sure you don't do anything about it. You know what will happen."

"You're an asshole."

"You're twelve."

Cary decided to stop talking before he shouted or did something equally irrational. Isaac seemed to have a very distinct talent for getting under Cary's skin.

ISAAC DIDN'T like crowds. Or parties. Especially parties filled with crowds of people who tended to view him like some sort of display at a zoo. Oh, look at Marigold Shelley's long lost feral grandson brought in from the wild. He looks awfully normal. Wonder if he bites? Isaac didn't want to be the talk of the town anymore, and he sure as hell didn't like all the Richie Riches of wine country looking at him like he was George of the Jungle.

I only have to deal with this until I get what I came for. It can't be long. His name had finally wandered out of the papers, and Marigold seemed to be getting closer to having his paperwork ready to go. He just… wanted out of this scene. Except he couldn't. Not yet.

"Hello, Isaac."

Fantastic. Another one.

"Hi." He tried to sound friendly. It was hard when the woman was peering at him as if he was a science experiment. She was younger than most of Marigold's friends. Probably one of the local wine makers who'd been invited since she lived in the area. He wondered if he'd met her before. Isaac wasn't very good at placing names with faces.

"Beverly. Remember? From the start of the season tasting?"

Beverly. Yes. Of course he didn't remember her. His job back then had been to charm everyone with his self-effacing shyness, not to remember potential business partners.

"Hello, Beverly. It's nice to see you again."

She gave him a shrewd smile. "You don't remember me, do you?"

"It's been a very hectic couple of months. I apologize."

"Don't worry. I don't mind. Apparently I used to chase you around my parents' vineyard when I was nine and you were a toddler. I don't remember doing that either, so no offense taken."

Isaac let out a laugh.

"Was it really hard? Growing up on the streets after you came from all this?"

Great. Questions. Isaac felt like he'd answered them about a million times already.

"I don't remember coming from all of this, so my time on the streets, well, it just is what it is, you know?"

"I can't imagine."

Isaac didn't want to talk about it anymore. Not at this point, not at the next one. Being ex-homeless seemed to be his calling card at these damn things. The people seemed to forget it had been a few years, that he'd been off the street since he was twenty. He'd been doing just fine when Marigold "found" him. He supposed that wasn't as good of a story, so they ignored that part.

"Hey, listen. I need to ask my grandmother something. Do you mind if I...." Isaac gestured to the other side of the room.

Marigold was in the middle of laughing at something one of her friends had said. She had her elbow perched on the mantle, and she looked radiant and really beautiful. Marigold was his exception to how much he hated these parties and the social scene in the wine country. If it wasn't for her, and obviously the promise of the trust fund, he'd have taken off after the first one and never returned. And the vineyard too. He loved working on the land and learning more about it. He was going to miss both of them when he left: Marigold and Falling River. But he was going to leave. Having a grandmother, even a fake one, and land he loved was appealing. Still. He'd have to be insane to want to be the cause of speculation for the rest of his life.

His shirt suddenly felt a little tight around his chest. His trousers, which had been altered to fit him perfectly, all of a sudden were a little restrictive. One of the women from town, this lady whom he'd talked to before, was coming toward him. Another one. Fantastic. She'd worn perfume, overwhelming and cloying, and she'd leaned closer to him the last time, like maybe he was some untamed jungle boy and she'd like to have her own sort of adventure on the other side of proper society. Isaac couldn't deal with her again. He didn't even want to try.

He had to escape.

The door out wasn't far if he didn't make eye contact with anyone and kept walking. It was only on the other side of the hors d'oeuvres table. Nobody would be in the kitchen with Gretchen and the assistant she'd hired for the night. Isaac slid along the wall, trying to look unobtrusive but not like a total weirdo. When he got to the arched doorway, he slid through and into the relative silence of Gretchen's kitchen. He took the backstairs to the second floor and collapsed against the hallway wall.

Freedom.

Isaac let out a long sigh of relief.

"What are you doing?" A sharp voice broke into his freedom. *Fucking hell can I have three seconds to myself?*

"Better question is, what are you doing? Why are you up here?"

"I followed you."

Cary didn't even look ashamed. Isaac was caught between anger and the desire to rip Cary's clothes off. Typical.

"Why? Did you think I was going to steal something again? Oh, wait, I never did in the first place. The sooner you get that in your head and leave me alone, the sooner I can figure out who the hell actually is doing it."

"I still don't trust you. I'm sure you don't find that surprising. You could be doing just about anything up here with the rest of the household distracted."

"I don't trust you either. Why does that mean you have to follow me? Go back down there. I don't want you here, and I'm not doing anything. Just escaping."

Cary made a frustrated growling noise and lunged for Isaac. Isaac thought he might be about to get a punch in the face but instead he had Cary, pinning him against the wall with an angry kiss.

"Why are you being such a pain in the ass about this?" Cary grumbled against his lips.

"Why did you screw my best friend over?"

Cary growled again and kissed harder, opening Isaac's mouth with his tongue. Isaac didn't want to want it, but he did. He reached up and pulled Cary's hair. Hard. Then he deepened the kiss and pressed his hips into Cary's.

"How do I know you're not up here because you're distracting me while your little assistant does something to make sure I get caught?"

"I'm up here because I want to be. Fuck." Cary slammed his lips into Isaac's and pulled his hair. It was almost too hard to be good but it was on the line between pleasure and pain. Isaac groaned into Cary's mouth.

"Hard for you to admit that you actually want it?"

"Shut up."

Cary kissed him again, roughly, like Isaac was quickly learning he liked it, with his body pressed against the wall and his thigh thick and muscled between Isaac's legs. Isaac let go of his anger and the hurt at being used, and let himself feel. Nobody had the power to get him as hot as Cary did in just a few seconds. He shuddered into Cary's touch. His head spun and his body felt all floaty, like it took everything he had just to stay anchored to the ground. Everything was a mass of hot dark kisses, Cary's thigh against his cock, where he wanted it most, hands cupping his face and pulling on his hair. It was too much to handle, but as always with Cary, nowhere near enough.

A glass broke at the bottom of the stairs. They pulled away from each other, panting. Shit. Somehow Cary had gotten under his skin. Again.

"I hate that I want you," Isaac grumbled.

"Come with me to the guesthouse," Cary said.

"What is this about?"

Cary hauled him in again. Isaac felt him, hard and insistent. He wanted him. "That. That's what it's about."

"Fuck. Fine. Why can't I say no to you?"

"We both want it. There's no shame in that."

Isaac frowned. "I don't want this."

Cary stepped back. "Okay." He turned to walk away, and that's when Isaac realized he did want it. He was just being stubborn. And hurt. He needed to grow up and take what he wanted.

"Cary. Wait."

Cary stopped and turned. "You going to change your mind again?"

"No. Fine. Damn it, let's go."

Isaac didn't let himself think anymore as he followed Cary down the stairs. He concentrated on the way Cary smelled and the echo of his touch. He had to get them out to the guesthouse before there could be more touches. Isaac worried he was going to get stuck talking, but they were in luck. The kitchen was empty, and they slipped out unnoticed.

It was dark in the guesthouse, the lights of the party a distant, unpleasant memory. He started stripping the moment they got inside.

"Not in the mood for romance, are you?"

Isaac didn't tell him he couldn't afford to want romance with Cary. That it was too much to ask and he knew it, so instead he only asked for what he could have. Which was still the hottest thing that had happened to him so far in his not-so-romantically-inclined life.

"I want you naked," Isaac said. "Take it off."

Cary looked a bit surprised at that, but he obliged, pulling his jacket off and stripping his shirt, trousers, and shoes just as quickly. Isaac liked being in charge. He remembered that from the night before last, right before things had gone to shit. Of how hot it was when he'd whispered dirty things in Cary's ears. It had been so hard to keep control that night. Isaac didn't even want to try.

Isaac slithered across the bed and flipped onto his belly. "Fuck me. Just like this." He arched his back and stretched.

"Jesus Christ, where did you come from?" Cary asked.

Isaac had no idea where this part of him came from. He'd never felt it before, but something about Cary drew it out. Cary crawled over him, dragging his lips up the center of Isaac's spine. He sucked on Isaac's neck hard, sure to leave a mark, and whispered hotly in his ear. "I want to taste you everywhere. I want to feel you around my tongue."

Isaac grabbed at his sheets. He wanted what Cary had just offered. He'd never had it before but he wanted Cary everywhere he could have him.

"Yes. *Please.*"

Cary kissed his way down Isaac's spine, leaving marks, Isaac was sure. It was agony waiting—delicious, high-strung agony. He wanted to feel Cary's mouth, his fingers, his cock. He wanted all of that at once, and the long moments of waiting for it were nearly painful.

When Cary finally pulled his cheeks apart, Isaac almost screamed. He hadn't even done anything yet, but the anticipation had him so on edge, he could've come thinking about it. Cary leaned closer, breathed on Isaac's entrance, and then took one long, slow lick through his crease. Isaac broke out in shivers. He'd always imagined it felt good, and it did. It was fucking amazing. Weird and wet and intimate, but perfect. Cary worked deeper with his tongue, getting everything slick, opening him up.

Isaac gripped the sheets and rolled his hips. He'd started babbling somewhere between the first exploratory lick and now, nonsense words and encouragement, breathless curses, and pleading moans.

"You want my fingers?" Cary asked.

"Yes. Fuck me now. Please."

Isaac was so lost in pleasure, he barely noticed Cary's lube-slicked fingers at his entrance, but he sure as hell felt them sliding in, thick, calloused, and substantial. Isaac groaned and pushed back, ready for the pressure.

"More," he moaned.

"You want me to push harder?"

"More," he repeated.

Cary built up speed with his fingers, using his tongue every once in a while to keep everything slick. It was heaven and torture. Isaac never wanted it to end. He didn't feel Cary move until his lips were on Isaac's neck, kissing and sucking little bites into it.

"I want you," Isaac moaned. He couldn't believe how far gone he was. He was spinning so hard it made him dizzy. Cary pushed at his prostate with two long fingers, rubbed it hard, and shifted his hard cock against Isaac's hip.

"You want me?"

"Yes. Now."

It felt odd and empty when Cary drew his fingers out. Isaac clenched on nothing and waited impatiently. He heard a wrapper rip, and then the faint squelch of Cary coating himself, and then he was back, thick head pushing right against Isaac's hole.

"You ready?"

"Hurry up. Fuck," Isaac said.

Cary chuckled breathlessly and pushed slowly until he was all the way in, belly, chest, thighs and pelvis plastered against Isaac's back.

"So damn good," Cary murmured. "So warm and soft and tight."

He started to roll his hips. It was familiar by then, even though they'd only had each other a handful of times. Cary's breath in his ear, and the smell of his skin, felt like a kind of home to him. Cary's rhythm made Isaac move, pushing his hips back to try and add to the friction, get the right kind of pressure. He got up on his elbows and pushed back, chasing the rush that was threatening to take him.

Cary's hand slid down Isaac's chest and around his cock, pulling gently, squeezing the head.

"Stop," Isaac breathed. "I'll come."

"Don't you want to?" Cary asked.

"Not yet. Still want you to fuck me." That probably didn't make sense, but it did to him. He didn't want it to be over. Any of it. And who knew how many times they had left? Maybe it was one more. Maybe this was it. He didn't want it to end.

"Come, babe. I'll make it happen again tonight. I promise."

Cary stroked harder, nailing Isaac's prostate again and again, his whispers of "hot and tight and so fucking beautiful" in Isaac's ear. Isaac was surrounded. He didn't have a chance.

He came hard, pulsing into Cary's hand, shouting in the dark. Cary stroked him through it, slow and steady, until he was reduced to a shivering pile of skin and sweat and bones.

"You okay?" Cary asked. He started to pull out.

"No. Stop. I'm good, finish here."

Cary stilled. "Are you sure?"

"Yeah."

Cary stroked again. Isaac was sensitive, and it almost hurt. But there was something raw and pleasurable about it. He wriggled back onto Cary's erection. Cary picked up the pace again for eight more strokes, maybe ten, and then he was shuddering against Isaac's back, teeth buried in Isaac's shoulder.

Isaac closed his eyes. Just for a second.

CHAPTER 10

CARY HAD spent most of the day dealing with the paperwork for the authentication of the Nine Sisters. He'd been in and out of town, "visiting" with the expert and basically jumping through a ton of hoops to make the next day's proceedings look as real as possible. He was exhausted. It was after dinner, which he'd missed, and all he wanted to do was collapse onto his bed and pass out. It didn't help he'd gotten about an hour of sleep the night before, a symptom of Isaac being in the room with him. Cary decided he didn't mind much as long as he got to do it again. Tomorrow night, perhaps, if everything went his way.

His phone buzzed insistently on his leg. It had been doing that all morning. And afternoon. And evening.

Jules. He remembered she had something she'd wanted to tell him the night before. Something he wasn't going to like. Cary wasn't in any more of a mood to hear something he wasn't going to like than he had been the night before. Seemed like his reprieve had finally run out. He couldn't avoid her forever.

"Jules. Sorry I couldn't get away last night to call." He tried to sound breathless, like she was catching him in the middle of something. He had a feeling she might not care anyway.

"Screw you, Talbot. I was up half the night worrying that you were dead somewhere."

Cary would've chuckled if she hadn't sounded like she was terrified. She probably wouldn't appreciate hearing he'd been up half the night as well. But not in danger. "I'm fine. Listen, we've got a bit of a problem."

"I'll say."

Cary didn't have the energy for her sass. He held up his hand tiredly and then realized she couldn't see him. "Wait, me first. Listen, Isaac didn't steal that stuff from Marigold. He's… one of us. He's after a trust fund, not a few necklaces and a tray. Those thefts are just as bad for him as they are for us."

"Wait. Isaac Shelley is a grifter?" Jules sounded as shocked as Cary had felt. Isaac really had managed to hide it from everyone, hadn't he? "Is he really Isaac Shelley?"

"Well, I'm not sure who he is. But essentially, yes. As long as Marigold accepts him as Isaac, he sure as hell is."

"Holy shit." Her voice sounded about like Cary's whole body had felt when he realized Isaac was into it just as deep as they were.

"That's kind of what I felt about it. But anyway, he's not stealing that stuff. I think we have a third player."

"Then you might not like my news even more."

"What is it?" Cary didn't even want to know. Best rip that bandage off quickly, then.

"I've been getting reports. People are saying the Black Mamba is nearby."

"Reports? Where do you get this stuff?"

"Like I'm going to tell you that. I never have. Why would I start now? Just know that I've heard rumors. They might not be true, but keep your eyes open. Hard."

"Fuck." Cary didn't have time to play games with the best player that there ever had been. Hopefully, wherever the Black Mamba was, they didn't cross paths. Cary doubted he was a match for someone like that.

"No kidding. Are you going to listen to me when I tell you to get out this time?" Jules asked. "All the signs are pointing toward the exit. Even you have to agree with me this time."

"Unfortunately, I do."

"So, pack up? I can be ready to go in an hour. We can be in Portland before lunch tomorrow."

"No. I'm not leaving right now. I need to figure out what the hell is going on."

Jules sighed loudly. "Why do you care what's going on? It's a mess, and we need to get the hell out before it gets worse. Are you trying to protect him? Is that what this is all about? Because you're going to end up in prison if you try to play the white knight. Those things never turn out well."

"It's not like that." But it was. He could barely admit it to himself, let alone admit it out loud. Cary didn't want to leave Isaac if the Black Mamba was around. For being what they were, the kid was awfully innocent. He wouldn't be able to handle himself around someone like that. He'd end up getting killed, or worse.

"Cary, you're an amazing liar, but you're no good at it when it comes to me. I know you care about Isaac. I can hear it in your voice. You still need to get out of there. Bring him with you if you want."

That sentence made a bolt of panic fly through him. "I want to see this through. Right here." Cary was being stubborn. And maybe Jules was a little bit right. His white knight seemed to be pushing through. And he didn't only want to protect Isaac. He wanted to protect Marigold too.

"You want to keep seeing Isaac."

Stop asking. I can't deal with you probing that much. Feelings had never been Cary's strong suit. Probably his weakest. It had taken him nearly a year to admit he loved Jules. Admitting he had feelings for Isaac after so little time was just… no. He couldn't.

"I told you what that was about. A little bit of fun and helpful to our cause. Besides, he's pretty. I like to look at him. That's all it is."

"Fantastic" came a dry voice from the door of his guesthouse. Isaac was standing there trying to look bored, but instead he looked hurt. More hurt than when he'd realized for the first time Cary was using him to convince Marigold to trust him.

Cary's heart clunked in his chest. His cheeks got hot. "I've gotta go, Jules."

"Get out of there."

"I need to go."

"You know, I never thought we were getting married anytime soon, but you could've been a little more flattering when you described me."

"Isaac—"

Isaac turned around and walked out. Cary had never felt that kind of panic, blind and weird and totally unexpected. He didn't know what to do with it. So he did the first thing he could think of. He ran to the door and shouted.

"Isaac, stop! Jesus. I didn't fucking mean it like that."

Isaac froze on the pool deck, feet from the door but farther from Cary than they'd been since they met. "I'm not sure I want to hear about it right now. I'm not sure I want to hear anything from you."

Isaac was angry, sure, but it was the hurt in his face when he walked away that really got to Cary. Fuck, he didn't want to hurt Isaac.

How have I gotten myself into this position so quickly? He cared about Isaac nearly as much as he cared about Jules, in a very different way obviously but no less real. No less tangible. In just a few days, the kid had managed to worm his way into Cary's heart.

Shit.

He pulled off the clothes he'd been in all day, the ones that were sweaty and hot and all of a sudden way too tight, and shoved his legs into his one pair of soft comfy sweats. He pulled on a T-shirt and shoved his feet into the flip-flops he always wore around his room, and followed Isaac. Cary was going to fix it. He'd never thought he'd come to Falling River and find whatever it was he had with Isaac, but he was going to fix it. He locked the guesthouse door and jogged across the pool deck. The main house was dark. Marigold had probably gone to sleep at least an hour before, but Cary slid through the kitchen door quietly. He turned for the backstairs and jogged up them silently.

He'd never been in Isaac's room, but the night before, he'd been in the hallway with him. He at least knew the general direction he was going. Cary crept across the landing and found himself in the small hallway they'd been in the night before. Most of the doors were shut, but one about three quarters of the way down was cracked open. A light shone out of the crack, and he could hear someone moving around. Cary decided to take a gamble. He seriously hoped he didn't end up running into Marigold in her nightie. That would probably be awkward.

It was Isaac, though, pacing, staring at the wall. He looked unhappy. Not like he'd been crying or anything, but unhappy. His hair was mussed, and he still had on his shorts and T-shirt. He looked gorgeous. Cary wanted to kiss him.

"Hey," Cary said quietly.

"Why are you in here?" Isaac didn't even turn around. He simply kept staring at the wall.

"I figured you and I needed to talk?" It sounded like a question. Cary supposed it was one.

"Why? What is there to talk about? I heard what you said to your friend. I'm just a bit of fun. I was here to help you convince Marigold and to be a bit of ass on the side. Even after we knew what each other was, it was still just a diversion for you. Or one for me. I still don't know what you fucking had planned for me."

"Isaac."

"What? I actually had feelings for you. Have. I know I'm stupid, and it's only been a few days, but I really like you. Even if it couldn't go anywhere, it was still more than a quick fuck for fun and to help me along the way. Maybe I'm just a dumb kid, and maybe I shouldn't have expected more out of you, but I did. Can't you just let me stew in my own stupidity in peace?"

"Isaac, be quiet. Marigold."

Isaac rolled his eyes. "Of course. Wouldn't want her to hear any of this. Don't worry. Her bedroom isn't even in this hallway. Unless she's standing right outside the door eavesdropping, she can't hear a thing we say."

"Okay."

"Part of me wishes she would. All of a sudden, I'd really like this job to just be over."

And that was partly Cary's fault. "Isaac. No, you don't. Just…." He didn't know what else to say.

"So. Why are you still here?" Isaac gave him a pointed look. "I'm not going to fuck you again just because you're bored, so if that's what you want, please take your ass back down to the guesthouse."

"It's not like that."

"Really? 'Cause it sure sounded like that's what you said earlier when you were talking on the phone."

Cary sighed. It was truth time. Cary fucking hated truth time, but Isaac deserved it. Isaac had just laid out all his cards. He should have honesty in return. "What you heard down there, that was me getting defensive, okay? I don't do feelings. Not usually, at least. You've managed to get to me, though, and I don't quite know what to do with it."

"Right. I think what you really mean to say is that I have your balls in my hands as far as Marigold is concerned and you want to stay on my good side. That is it, isn't it?"

"Isaac, things don't look so good for you either. You say you didn't steal that stuff, and I believe you, but your name is on those papers. One of the fences said he recognized your picture. It's not just my ass on the line here. Remember that."

"He was lying. I was never there."

"Yeah, but Marigold doesn't know that. Listen. We could easily fuck this up for each other. Hard-core. End up in jail for a long goddamn time. We both know that. Is that what you want?"

"No." Isaac looked mutinous.

"Look at me. You know when I'm trying to be charming and when I'm telling the truth. I do have feelings for you. I have since the first time we kissed. I just… can't have feelings for you. It's dangerous. But I do."

"You don't think it's way more dangerous for me? I'm in this alone. I don't have an assistant somewhere making sure things work out for me, and apparently it's very easy to pull one over on me."

"You don't have to be in this alone."

"Right again. Why would you help me?"

Cary sighed. "You're really not hearing me. Because I like you. A lot. Someone's trying to frame you, and I'm going to assume because a bottle of wine disappeared they're trying to frame me as well. Maybe they're not, but it's always good to be cautious. We're better in this together, you know."

"I don't know that I want to be in anything together with you. You hurt me. You screwed Roman over. I can't trust you."

"You can. This isn't like the thing with Roman. He and I were after the same prize. You and I aren't. Plus, I didn't know him. I already said how I feel about you."

"I'm not sure."

Cary nodded. Those little words hurt like hell. He *never* offered help. He never put himself out there like that. To do it and only get a wary answer in return sucked more than he would've thought. Cary tried to pretend his gut hadn't been churning for the entire conversation.

"That's fine. I'll be down in my room if you change your mind. I'm not going to do anything to you, Isaac. I'm not going to ruin this for you. Not just because I don't want you telling Marigold about me, but because I don't want to hurt you. We can be separate but in accordance. I'm okay with that, I guess. If you want more, though, I'm happy to give it."

Isaac sighed. "I don't want to do anything to hurt you either. And that annoys me to say probably more than it annoys you not to want to hurt me."

It was probably the weirdest conversation Cary had ever had.

"I'm fine with that as long as we stick to the original plan. I take the trust, you take the Nine Sisters. Other than the wines, I don't want you conning anything from Marigold."

"Wasn't going to. You really care about her, don't you?"

"Apparently caring about people when I shouldn't is one of my fatal flaws. It's probably going to get me in a hell of a lot of trouble someday."

"I like that you care. It might get you in trouble, but it could just as easily get you out of it too."

Isaac stared at him. "You really aren't going to end this for me?" His face was still wary, like he didn't dare believe.

Cary's belly ached. He couldn't take it. He walked over and cupped Isaac's face in his hands. "I'm really not going to. I. Fuck. I feel…." Cary was done talking. He needed to show.

He lowered his mouth to Isaac's in a soft kiss. It wasn't like any of the other kisses. There wasn't any heat, no desperation, not even any calculated effort to get a certain response. It was just Cary showing Isaac he fucking cared. As much as he didn't want to. He bit gently at Isaac's lower lip, trying to get him to participate. Isaac sighed into Cary's mouth. He slid his arms up and over Cary's shoulders and connected his hands behind Cary's neck.

"Okay. I believe you," Isaac finally said after the kiss slowly died.

"You believe that I care about you and I'm not going to hurt you?"

"Yeah."

Finally. After all that damn talking, all it had taken was a kiss. Cary wished he'd kissed him a long time before he'd spilled his guts. "Okay. Good. So then what's the next step?"

"I need to figure out who's framing me. Then I think we take them out."

Cary liked the sound of "we" more than he could have said. "We take them out. Sounds like a good plan to me."

"Do you want to just stay up here tonight?"

"Yeah. I, um, already locked the guesthouse door so I don't need to go back down there."

Isaac raised his eyebrows. "Presumptuous much?"

Cary pinched him on the side. "Hopeful. Just hopeful."

CARY WOKE up in Isaac's bed to the sound of something knocking in the front of the house. He was disoriented for a moment, in the bright yellow room he didn't recognize, but then he saw the warm pale body next to him and remembered. He was upstairs. The question then was what was going on downstairs?

"What the hell?" he said quietly and sat up in bed. Isaac made a few sleepy noises and reached for Cary's waist.

"What's going on?" he asked. He was clearly barely awake.

"I don't know. Someone's out front." Cary swung his legs over the side of the bed and dragged his sweats over his legs and put his flip-flops on. "Stay up here, 'kay? I'll go check it out and see if Marigold's okay."

"Mmph." Isaac flopped on his pillow. He stayed there for a good ten seconds before he sat up suddenly. He looked warily at Cary. "Where are you going? Walk of shame?"

"No." Cary smiled and brushed Isaac's hair off his face. "You really didn't hear any of what I just said to you?"

Isaac shook his head. "No. Did I seem awake?"

"Not really," Cary whispered. "Be quiet. There are noises outside."

"You want me to come with you?"

"Just get dressed. Quietly. I'll be out in the hallway."

Cary slipped out of the bedroom and tiptoed to the landing over the main room. It was already bright in the early morning, but mostly silent. Marigold was standing by the front door in her robe and slippers. Three uniformed policemen were on the other side, and they didn't look happy. Marigold looked only mildly unamused but mostly just tired.

"Ma'am, we got a domestic disturbance call from this address. We'll need to do a sweep of the property to make sure that everyone is okay," said one of the policemen. He was beefy and thick-necked. Cary wouldn't have wanted to be stuck with him in a dark alley. Marigold didn't seem fazed by him, though. She simply shook her head.

"There really is no need. That call must've been a mistake. Everyone in the house is asleep but me. They have been asleep all night, and they're still asleep. I was just about to make tea. I can assure you I didn't make any phone calls to the police."

"The call originated from a cell phone at this address. Are you certain there hasn't been anything going on here?" The policeman stuck his head into the house and craned it around. Cary jerked behind the corner so he couldn't be seen. Not that the policemen could or would do anything to him, but a lifetime of paranoia wasn't easy to forget.

Marigold chuckled. "Can you hear anything? I don't hear anything."

In that moment a loud whistle came from the direction of the kitchen. Cary felt a warm presence behind him, and he jumped a little before he realized it was Isaac. Well other than uniformed police officers questioning Marigold. That was a bit of a problem.

"What the hell. Why are there police here?" he whispered. Cary turned to look at him.

Isaac looked a little freaked out. Cary was only freaking out a tiny bit. Just a little. He was honestly about to have a heart attack. The police. In Marigold's house. What if they figured out he wasn't supposed to be there?

Don't be irrational. They're local police, not the FBI. They have nothing to do with you. It's just a misunderstanding.

"I have no fucking clue. I guess someone called in a domestic disturbance. Marigold is telling them that nothing's going on, but they're trying to search the property to make sure everything is okay. Do you have anything on you that could get you in trouble?"

"No. At least I don't think so." Isaac made a face. "Of course, there's a good chance that I fucking do. Someone called the police here, right? What if something else has been stolen? I need to check in my room and make sure I don't 'have' anything." Isaac shivered.

Whoever was playing games with them may have just upped their level.

"I'm going to go with you. Marigold is telling the cops everyone's asleep. Let's go disappear. It looks like she has this, and we need to make sure you don't have anything in case they search the property."

"You want to leave her alone with them?"

"They're not going to hurt her. They're police officers. She's the owner of the house, and she's harmless. Let's go make sure there's nothing in your room," he repeated. He had to get Isaac moving. "I'm fairly sure she's going to be able to get them to go away, but if she can't, it's better to be safe."

Isaac considered that for a moment and then nodded. They scurried back to Isaac's room. When they got there, Isaac took the closet, and Cary looked through the drawers in his dresser.

"Nothing in here," Isaac reported.

"It's all clear in here too. I'll look under the bed."

"No, it's—"

Cary had already dived and was scanning the floor under the bed. He picked up the mattress just to be safe and… oh.

Isaac put his face in his hands. "Fuck. That's embarrassing. I think I'll just sink into the carpet now."

One bottle of lube and one rather sparkly purple vibrator were nestled under the mattress. Cary snorted to hide the fact that he'd turned a rather bright shade of pink. "Really?"

Isaac brought his hands away from his face and looked at Cary. "What? It had been months. I was out here with a bunch of chicks and one middle-aged straight dude until you came."

Cary grinned. "So you like toys, huh?"

"Mostly out of necessity, but they can be fun." Isaac didn't want to talk about it. That much was obvious. Cary couldn't resist one more little jab.

"I guess it's too bad it's not Christmas time. I have a few gift ideas in mind." He chuckled.

"Jesus. You're not going to drop this, are you?"

"Probably not. But you should also not keep that where the housekeeper could find it if they decide to flip the mattress. Underwear drawer is better."

"She does my laundry. And puts it away."

Cary laughed. "Must be a tough life you've been living here."

"It's fucking awkward, though. I tried to do my own laundry at first, but they just kept taking it away from me."

"Well, if you can't keep it in your underwear drawer like any other self-respecting person, maybe I should confiscate this thing."

Isaac pushed the mattress out of Cary's hand. It flopped onto its base with a soft *thump*. "Knock it off. You know, we should go see if Marigold's okay."

Cary agreed. "And to be quite honest, after the wine incident, I should make sure there aren't any gifts hiding in my room too."

"You don't seem to be framed for stealing like I have been. At least not yet. But it's probably still a good idea."

They found Marigold in the kitchen by herself, nursing a warm cup of tea.

"What was that?" Isaac asked when they'd sat down at the table next to her. "I was going to come help, but I figured it was best if you handled it on your own since nobody around here has quite decided to trust me yet."

Marigold snorted. "That was our local police, who obviously have nothing better to do. They were going to search the house. I told them to go grab some donuts and coffee on their way back to the station. Domestic disturbance," she huffed. "The closest we've had to a domestic disturbance around here was when Sultan wouldn't leave Cupcake alone in her pen."

Isaac smiled.

"Sultan's kind of a Romeo, and he learned how to unlatch the old locks in the stable. They had to relatch all the doors with new hardware to keep him away from his ladylove. She's so not into him."

"I'm glad everything's okay."

"Yes. You two should go back to bed for a little while. It's awfully early. I can't imagine why anyone would be fighting at this hour. Or doing anything other than sleeping."

Cary noticed she hadn't said anything about the fact that he was in her grandson's bedroom. She didn't seem to mind at all.

"I think I will hit the sack for a little while longer," Cary muttered. "But I want to grab my glasses first. They're in my bed in the guesthouse."

"You don't need your glasses if you're going to shut your eyes, dear." Marigold shooed him upstairs. Cary felt like that was a little odd. What did she care if he went to get his glasses? "If you spend time looking for them, you'll have been up long enough that you won't want to go back to sleep. Just go. You can get them the next time you two wake up."

Oh. She was matchmaking. Again. Jesus. Marigold wanted them in the same bed as much as they both did. Isaac raised his eyebrows and shrugged. He followed Cary up the stairs until they were back in his room, collapsed on the bed.

"Your grandmother needs a boyfriend," Cary mumbled.

"Apparently she's happy enough trying to find me one." Isaac said with a slightly annoyed smile. "She's not very subtle about it."

"No kidding. Maybe she thinks subtlety takes too much time."

Cary wrapped his arms around Isaac's waist and squiggled his hands up under the T-shirt Isaac had dragged on. He liked Isaac's skin. It helped him sleep.

"Wake us up in like an hour?" Isaac asked.

"Sure thing."

CHAPTER 11

A COUPLE of hours later, Cary was in the middle of rooting around on the floor for the green shirt he knew he'd had on the day before when nearly tripped over a roll of what felt like canvas. Stiff, painted canvas tied with an old piece of hemp rope. What the hell? Cary grabbed it and pulled it out of his bag. Definitely not his. Definitely old. Definitely weird. Cary's pulse raced in his chest. He was suddenly nervous as hell. He thought of all the stolen objects, thought of the cops who had been here that morning, and tried not to let his imagination get to him.

Just see what it is.

He pulled the door to the guesthouse shut and locked it. Then he shut the blinds for good measure. Paranoid? Maybe. But he had just found some old painting in his belongings. What was that they said about paranoia? You weren't paranoid if you were right? Close enough. Well, it definitely looked like Cary was right about something. He took a deep breath and unrolled the canvas. What he saw made his mouth dry.

It was a painting, which he'd already known it was going to be. What kind of painting, well, that was the part that made him feel like he was going to throw up.

It wasn't one that he'd ever seen before, and he'd be willing to bet not many people had. But the style? It was unmistakable. Cary would have recognized it anywhere in the world. He scanned the canvas until he found what he was looking for. Right there in the corner, woven into the man's abstract hat. Cary swore out loud. Jesus.

Somehow, and fuck if he knew how, stuck in the bottom of Cary's duffel bag for who knew how many days was a fucking Picasso. And the police had just been out front.

Cary would've been so fucking screwed he wouldn't have seen the light of day for the rest of his life. A Picasso. He was standing in Marigold's guesthouse holding a goddamn priceless piece of art by one of the great masters. His vision went a little wavy.

Marigold didn't have a Picasso, did she? Cary racked his brain trying to think of one. He would've noticed if it had been in any of the rooms he'd been in. Not just anyone had beyond priceless, world-famous art hanging in their house. He'd have noticed. Anyone would. But the Picasso had come from somewhere. And that was the part that Cary needed to figure out before the cops came again.

Cary quickly rolled the painting up and tied it with the crude hemp rope. It felt wrong, like he should be handling the damn thing with gloves and tongs rather than shoving a rope around it, but he didn't have the equipment to deal with it correctly. Cary wondered how many millions he had in his uncovered hands. He couldn't even fathom it. He'd rather not think about it, to be honest. He slid the painting back into his duffel bag and zipped it to be safe.

Back at the main house, he jogged upstairs, bag and painting in his hand. There was no way in hell he was letting the damn thing out of his sight.

"Isaac?" Cary said when he got back into the room.

"Everything okay?"

Cary made a strangled noise. "No. Everything is definitely not okay." He gestured with his face toward his duffel bag.

"What's in there?" Isaac looked like he almost didn't want to know. Cary totally felt his pain. He didn't want to know either. In fact, if he could get rid of the damn thing, he would. There was fencing some old expensive wine, and then there was trying to unload a fucking hot Picasso that was probably on about a million lists in a million government agencies.

"I'm going to show you. I'm pretty damn sure it wasn't there yesterday, and I'm very sure it's not mine. I'm also thinking the cops weren't an accident."

"Okay. Breathe. Just show me."

"Fucking hell." Cary gingerly pulled the painting from his bag and unrolled it. "If anyone catches me with this damn thing, I'm going to be in so much trouble."

"Holy shit. Is that what I think it might be?" Isaac asked. Cary saw him scanning for a signature too. He almost laughed at Isaac's face when he found it, but it wasn't funny. Nothing about the last twenty minutes had been funny.

"You think this is a forgery?"

"I don't know. If it is, it's very good. Good enough that had the police been looking for anything, that would've got me brought in for some strenuous questioning, at least." Cary sighed. "At the rate things are going with the stolen goods and what Jules told me, I'm guessing it's not."

"What did Jules tell you?"

They'd so busy arguing and making up, he hadn't had a chance to tell Isaac. "The Black Mamba's in town."

"You think that's what this—?"

Cary didn't know anything anymore. Not a damn thing. "I can't see why. The Black Mamba doesn't even know me."

"But if the police were going to look through people's stuff? I can see the setup there."

"Again, why? The Black Mamba doesn't even know who I am."

"Yeah, but I've been sleeping in that room. What if it's my fault?"

Cary reached out and cupped Isaac's face. "I never thought this was your fault. Not for a second."

"What are we going to do?"

There was that "we" again. Cary liked it.

"Well, I think I have a starting place at least. There's someone I'd like you to meet."

Isaac stared at Cary warily. "Who is it?"

"Actually, you've met her before. I just thought it was time to make it official. Jules, my assistant. I need her to take a look at this and see what she can come up with, and I figured you'd probably like to join me."

Cary just about died at the thought of driving around with a fucking Picasso in his car, but he really didn't have much choice.

"Hell, yes. I want to know what the hell is going on just as much as you do."

"Okay. You'll have to tell Marigold something, obviously. Lunch?"

"Lunch sounds good. I could go for another burrito anyway."

"If they're always as good as last time, I could go for another one of those." That was, if he managed to make it through the rest of the morning with his innards intact. He'd felt nauseated since he unrolled the painting in his room.

Cary grimaced and went to wrap the priceless painting up and stick it in his gym bag. As if that didn't make him feel like his heart was about to palpitate out of his chest. Picasso. Fucking hell. He turned for the door, and Isaac held him back. "Cary?"

"What's up?"

Isaac lunged forward and took Cary's mouth in a long kiss. It helped somehow to center him when he felt like he wanted to fly off the rails. Whatever it was, Cary was grateful.

"Um, that's up. I wanted to kiss you."

"Thank you." Cary brushed one more kiss across Isaac's lips. "I'm more than all right with kissing. But please don't crush the painting."

"Sorry." Isaac smiled shyly at the ground. It was something he did. It drove Cary insane. He wanted to pull Isaac back in for about a hundred more kisses, maybe some clothing removal. Well, everything to be honest. But they had things to do and priceless paintings to hide as far away from Falling River as possible.

"Okay, we'd better go."

The trip into town was much more comfortable than the last one they had taken. Isaac snuck his hand over and cupped Cary's thigh while he drove. They both kept their eyes on the painting in the duffel bag, but their hands were reserved for each other. It felt good to have that kind of touch, even if Cary had never thought it would. Isaac was sweet and soft and oddly innocent. Cary had no idea how he'd ever gotten mixed up with Roman. Roman was a good guy, but he was tough on the outside. Tanned and leathery hard from years in the game. He seemed to have had a soft spot for Isaac, though, if he'd set him up with such a perfect job.

"Jules has a room in one of the highway hotels just outside of town."

"Has she been stuck out there the whole time?" Isaac made a face. "That's so boring. We should bring her back with us."

"Boring but necessary. She runs tech and does about a million things I have no idea how to do. And how are we going to bring her back with us? Marigold doesn't even know she exists."

Isaac shrugged. "We'll think of something, I guess. How'd you two end up together?"

Cary laughed. "It's a long story. Probably one not too different than you and Roman, actually. She was in trouble, she was just a kid, she needed someone to help her out of it. That was a few years ago, but she's been with me ever since."

"Aw, you rescued her like a white knight?"

"Yes, and led her into a life of crime. Very chivalrous of me."

"My guess is whatever she was doing before was getting her into enough trouble. She probably didn't really need much help from you to find more."

That was just about the most accurate description of Jules that Cary had ever heard. Trouble was irresistible to her. "You would be correct," Cary said. "She loves pretty, shiny things and finding her way into places she has zero business being in. A perfect match for me really. Once she has me in, I can charm people out of just about anything."

"No kidding."

Cary didn't miss the look Isaac gave him. The wines. He'd nearly forgotten them in the excitement of the morning. Jesus. He should've dropped it when Jules told him the first time. He almost didn't have the heart to go through with his con anymore. Everything had changed when that painting showed up in his room.

"Hey, don't worry about that. Let's deal with our magically appearing masterpiece first, okay?"

"Sure. I'm kind of interested to talk to Jules more," Isaac admitted.

"I'm sure she'll be happy to give you lots of information. Probably far too much."

Isaac chuckled and leaned his head against the headrest. "I hope me being there doesn't freak her out."

"Nah. She's pretty hard to freak out. And if she does, well that's nothing that a huge latte and a few baked goods won't cure."

Isaac smiled into the bright golden light of the morning.

They showed up in the room armed with three very large lattes and blueberry muffins for everyone. Jules was in her typical spot, running the world with dictator-like precision behind her bank of computers.

"Hey, boss—ohh. What have we here?"

"Jules, Isaac. Isaac, Jules. Like I said, he didn't steal all that stuff."

Jules raised her eyebrows.

"I didn't," Isaac added. "We need to figure out who's been doing that."

"We also need to figure out who planted this in my stuff and called the cops. It's lucky that Marigold told them there wasn't anything wrong, or they could've easily found this. I highly doubt it would've looked very good. I'd probably be on my way to some very unfriendly prison right about now."

"What's 'this'?" Jules looked alarmed.

"Why don't you take a look?" Cary pulled the rolled-up painting from his duffel and handed it to her. "Careful with that thing. I don't even want to know what it's worth."

Jules gingerly unrolled the painting. She stared for a few long minutes before she let out a rough breath. "Fuck. Is this what I think it is?" Like Isaac earlier, it seemed she didn't want to believe what she was looking at.

"If you think it's a Picasso, then yes. You would be correct."

Jules looked like she was about to drop the damn thing. Cary didn't blame her. His reaction hadn't been much better. He was still afraid to touch it with his bare hands. "A real one?" Jules whispered.

"I'm only so-so when it comes to art forgery, but as far as I can tell, yes. It's very, very real."

"Fuck," she said again.

Cary couldn't agree with her more.

"We are sitting in an economy room in the Sunshine Inn with a fucking Picasso. How the hell do you have this?"

"Like I said, I don't know, and I probably don't want to know. It was planted in my stuff. My guess is someone wanted me to get caught with it. What I need you to do is figure out exactly what painting that is and who is supposed to have it. If it's been recently stolen, I'm in a world of trouble."

"Yeah. No problem."

Isaac looked at Cary with eyes wide. "She can just do that?"

Jules shot Isaac a sassy look, as usual. It warmed Cary's heart to see Isaac getting the same disrespectful treatment he always did. "Yes," Jules snapped. "*She* can do that."

It took about an hour, with Isaac and Cary pacing and drinking coffee, sitting on the bed, hands clasped, and yeah, Jules noticed that, before she finally said, "Jesus fucking Christ. I found it. I don't know why I didn't look there first."

"She likes to swear, doesn't she?" Isaac asked.

Cary laughed. "Yes. She does."

"What is it, Jules?"

"Something worth swearing over. This painting does show up on a list. A very… specialized list."

"And what list is that?"

She swallowed a couple of times before she spoke. It wasn't like Jules to get that nervous. Cary figured it was a bad sign.

"The list that Interpol and FBI's art crimes divisions both have in their databases. The supposed, um, conquests of one rather infamous Black Mamba."

"Jesus fucking Christ." No. No, no, no. Cary did not want to be on the Black Mamba's hit list and it looked like that's exactly what had happened. That painting was a plant. Cary just had to figure out why.

"That's exactly what I thought," Jules said.

Isaac sat there silently for a long time. "Wait, so what you're saying is that painting is something the Black Mamba stole and somehow it's been planted on Cary?"

"You're a quick one, kid." Jules clearly wasn't freaked out enough to lose her sarcasm. At least some things in the world remained the same.

"I bet I'm older than you."

Jules snorted. "Yes, then. That's what it means."

"And the Black Mamba then...."

"Is near enough to plant this on Cary, which we already knew, and the guy either has it in for Cary or has decided that he's a convenient scapegoat."

Isaac shook his head. "But the Black Mamba isn't even a guy. Black Mamba is a woman. I guess the authorities don't know that, so Cary could get framed just as easily either way, but if she'd wanted him arrested, he'd already be gone. What is this? I don't get it."

"Wait." Cary stared at Isaac. "How the hell do you know that? Nobody knows a damn thing about this person. How did you know it was a woman?"

"Roman knew her. Well, he met her a few times at least. He just said, well, that she was a she. And that she was the reason he had to get out of the states."

"Damn." Just like Isaac had said: if she wanted him gone, he'd have been there already.

"Right? So this was just a game. She expected Cary to find the painting, not the cops. Why is she messing with us? We're nothing to her."

"Apparently that's not true."

"Guys." Isaac bit his lip. "Guys. What if the Black Mamba is Kitty?"

CHAPTER 12

ISAAC HAD had a bad feeling about Kitty since the very first day he'd walked into Falling River. Sure, she didn't like him, but it wasn't just that. There was something about her that felt off. What if it was that? What if the greatest grifter and art thief in the world had been under his nose the whole time, and he'd never known it? The thought of that made him a little sick. But at the same time, as much as he didn't like her, he had to admit to a grudging respect. She'd gotten away with some seriously amazing cons. And probably a hell of a lot more of them that nobody knew about.

"What makes you think it's Kitty?" Jules asked. "I know you guys have issues with her, but is she Black Mamba material?"

Cary chuckled. "We can't just blame it on her because she's, like, the most unpleasant woman who's ever existed?"

Jules chuckled. "Tempting as it is, that's exactly why you can't blame it on her. There's no way she's the Black Mamba. She'd be a hell of a lot better than that. I haven't had up-close-and-personal experience with her like you have, but even I know Kitty is too unpleasant to be a good grifter. She'd never manage half of what the Black Mamba has supposedly done."

"Well, there aren't that many choices at the vineyard. I suppose we just need to break it down. Shouldn't take too long."

"So do we know for sure it's the Black Mamba who is trying to frame you two?"

"Yes," Cary said. "Nobody else would have access to that Picasso unless the FBI is wrong about who has it, or Mamba has an assistant."

"Not likely," Jules muttered. "Someone like that works alone."

"So, again. Let's look at who we have."

"Mike," Cary started.

"Black Mamba is a woman," Isaac said again.

"Roman said Black Mamba is a woman. We don't know that for sure."

"He had no reason to lie. But anyway, Mike's supposedly been there since right after the real Isaac's parents died. There's no way he'd be doing this. He's just an employee, and he's been there forever."

"Are you sure it's not because you like him?"

"I'm sure. I'm pretty good at reading people, present company excluded. Plus, he's got a wife and two kids, and a very long-term job that takes up a lot of his time. When would he have the time to pull of heists and cons?"

"True," Cary agreed.

"Okay, then there's the farmers who work for Mike, and Jose, Kitty's assistant," Isaac ticked off.

"All male?" Jules asked.

"Yes, and all with too many work hours and little or no access to the main house. For the moment, can we leave them out of the picture? Let's assume Roman was right."

Cary nodded. "So there's Kitty, Tilly who works in the press and the barrel room, right? Gretchen, the housekeeper, and Marigold herself."

Isaac snorted. "It's not Gretchen. She spends all day cooking. When would she have time to be a master con artist? Besides, she's been around for a long time."

"The housekeeper?"

"Same. Since I was a kid apparently. Marigold says she's one of the ones who recognized me right away."

"Tilly?"

Isaac shrugged. "I have literally never seen her at the house. I've hardly seen her at all honestly. She comes to work and goes home. I think she's married too, but I haven't even talked to her many times."

"And that leaves our best friend, Kitty. How long did Marigold say she's been at the vineyard?"

"About a year. Since Ralph, the old manager, retired, I guess."

"That's a lot of investment into a con. But let's say she was trying to get Marigold to sign Falling River over to her since she managed it. It would be in her best interests to get rid of you."

"But why is she messing with you?"

"You recognized me after a while. Who's to say that Kitty didn't? If she is who we think she is. I don't think I ran into her ever, but that doesn't mean I didn't."

Isaac sighed. "I cannot believe that Kitty—lame, bitchy Kitty—is the Black Mamba. That would be such a letdown. Is she even old enough?"

Cary nodded. "Kitty has to be at least in her late thirties. She's old enough. The Black Mamba has only been operating for about fifteen years that we know of. Kitty's definitely old enough."

"But what would she want with Marigold's vineyard? Isn't there enough out there in her secret bat-lair for her to live happily for at least three lifetimes?"

Jules chuckled. "If these Interpol and white-collar crime lists are enough to go by, she doesn't need a thing from Falling River. She could buy and sell it about six times over."

"Maybe there's just something there that she really wants."

"Jules, can you find anything on Kitty?"

Jules shook her head. "Not yet. I've been looking for her since you started talking. She's a ghost."

"So you're saying Kitty St. Clair isn't her real name?"

Jules laughed out loud. "Did you really think it was?" She must've noticed Isaac and Cary staring at her without laughing. "No. It's not. Whatever she's doing, that much is certain."

"Damn. So it could be her."

"And she's after everything Marigold has. Hell, no." Isaac looked like he wanted to growl. "I can't believe I've spent so much time underneath the same roof as her. She went after Roman because he pissed her off. Now she's going after Marigold too."

"And she'd have the perfect cover. The vineyard manager would have lots of excuses to travel. Conferences, meetings with other vintners. She could be anywhere she wanted half the time, and nobody would be the wiser."

"Fucking Kitty. I knew I didn't like her."

"We need to get her out of there. She could be hurting Marigold as we speak."

Cary shook his head. "I know you want to protect Marigold, Isaac, but think about it. As long as Marigold hasn't signed anything over to her yet but it looks like she possibly might stop trusting you, then Kitty won't do anything. Marigold will be safe. She can't make any definite moves, though. That's when things'll get dangerous for her."

"We have to go." Isaac looked panicked. Cary needed to calm him the hell down before he did something to get them all in a lot of trouble.

"What I'm saying is, it's not going to happen right now. I think the Picasso was a warning. Stay out of her business. I think what she's doing to you? That's not a warning. That's her wanting you gone. So we need to work on undermining her with Marigold. Get her out of there."

"Why can't I just tell Marigold?"

"It'll be your word against hers. You are her grandson, but she's known Kitty longer."

"Then what do we do?"

Cary shrugged. "I happen to know where the necklace is that Marigold lost. What if we also happen to find it in Kitty's stuff?"

"Then Marigold will accuse her of stealing it and fire her?"

Cary nodded. "Does that plan work for you?"

"Yes. I like it. Make it easy for her to choose. Cut and dried. Kitty stole from her."

"Only problem is, we're going to have to buy Marigold's necklace back from Sandro. You have any cash reserves?"

"Yeah. Roman left me with quite a bit of operating capital."

"Good. You're going to need it. Jules, can you contact Sandro and let him know we'd like to make a purchase?"

Jules nodded.

"Good. Isaac and I have some driving to do."

Later that night, the two of them were on the way back from San Francisco. The drive wasn't super long, but it was hot and dusty, and the air conditioner in Cary's rented car wasn't the best. Isaac had Marigold's necklace in his pocket. Sandro had bled them dry for the damn thing, but Cary thought it was worth it in the end. At least it would be for Isaac. He didn't know what was going to happen with him and the Nine Sisters. With the Black Mamba in play, he wondered if he'd better abort the whole damn thing. Too bad about what he spent getting the wine back. Better to lose a couple grand than end up dead.

"I'm going to enjoy getting that wench ousted," Isaac muttered. "Ten grand. Ten fucking grand."

"Well, guess who got to buy back the wine she stole. That kind of hurt too."

Isaac cringed. "Sorry about that. How much?"

"Seven."

"For a bottle of wine? I don't know why I'm even surprised after spending all week down there. I'm seriously going to enjoy this."

They didn't wait long. Once they got in, it was time to get the plan started. They thought it best to have Isaac talk to her, show her the necklace, and slowly spit out the story. Isaac hoped he was convincing enough to sell it.

Marigold was sitting in her sunroom with a book and a cup of tea. She looked so sweet and trusting, Isaac hated to be pulling yet another con on her. But it was for her own good, right? She had to get rid of Kitty. They couldn't tell her the truth, so this was the best way.

"Hey, Marigold. I mean Grandmother." Isaac was blushing already. Fantastic start. Great. He concentrated on calming down. It was fine to look a little bit nervous, but it wasn't good to look like he was lying. *Calm down. Calm.*

"Yes, dear. How are you?" She looked up from her book and smiled. "Hello, Cary. I didn't know you were with him."

"Yes." Cary smiled and nudged Isaac gently. Cary had told him it was better if he did it alone, but Isaac didn't think he could. He needed Cary there to get through it. Fantastic grifter he was.

Get it over with. Make her believe it.

"Um, I have something a little uncomfortable to tell you, and I wanted Cary with me because I figured it might be better if another person knew about it. Just in case."

Isaac thought he was doing pretty well: innocent, unsure, awkward. The last one was true anyway. He hated dealing with this shit.

"What's up?" she asked.

Isaac nearly smiled. He loved how casual Marigold was. "So, I was in the main offices with Mike this morning for a little while after Cary and I left the house, and he asked me if I'd grab a stapler, right?" That part was true. They'd stopped there for a few moments to make sure Kitty was safely where she belonged.

Marigold smiled encouragingly. "Okay. What happened?"

"So I couldn't find his or the one on Jared's desk in the main room. I saw that Kitty had one, and I went in there to grab it. It's just a stapler. I didn't think she'd mind. But when I went to get it, I knocked a few things over, and one of them was a box. The box fell to the ground and opened, and… well." Isaac dug in his pocket. "I think you might recognize what was in it."

It was Marigold's necklace. He watched her face dawn in happiness. "My necklace. You found it."

"Yeah. Maybe Kitty was taking it to get cleaned for you, or repaired or something. But, well, I don't know. I just wanted to let you know so you could deal with it however you wanted to deal with it."

"Thank you, Isaac, darling."

"You think she stole it?" He wanted to put the idea in Marigold's head. Maybe she'd already had it herself, but it didn't hurt to be too safe.

Marigold's face flashed with irritation. "Well, she sure didn't mention that she was getting it cleaned for me when I was talking about how it was missing. And she also didn't mention it when I was digging around the house looking for it. I'll give her a chance to explain, but as far as I'm concerned, if she stole it...." Marigold shrugged dismissively.

"What are you going to do?" Isaac asked.

"Fire her, obviously. I can't have staff members who steal things from me. Maybe she has my earrings too. I've been looking around for them. I know I put them back in my jewelry box the last time I wore them."

"I'm really sorry, Grandmother. I know you like to be able to trust people." Isaac was dancing inside. Had it worked? Please let Kitty not have an explanation. Please let her be gone. Isaac was sure it was her who'd been screwing with him. She'd never liked him. It had to be her. This had to work.

"It's fine. I just—I hate dealing with this kind of stuff."

Isaac tried to look sympathetic when he was doing the can-can in his head. "Do you want me to be there with you?"

Marigold sighed. "Might as well. Maybe I'll find her later this afternoon. She should be back from her business in town by then, right."

Isaac wondered if she was in town selling something else she'd stolen and tried to pin on him.

"Yeah. Hopefully."

"KITTY, I need to speak with you," Marigold said.

Isaac cringed. He'd offered to be there, but it didn't mean he was eager to watch this happen. Well, okay, a little bit of him was, but still. He'd framed Kitty to get rid of her, not because he was going to enjoy watching her squirm. Much.

"What is it, Marigold?" Kitty looked up from her desk. Maybe she was there planning her next frame job. Her sour face was enough for Isaac to lose some of his sympathy. He really didn't like her.

"I found something this morning. I believe you know exactly where I found it." Marigold pulled the necklace out from beneath the collar of her shirt and let it fall.

Kitty's face turned red for a moment and anger flashed across it before she schooled it into a pleased smile. "I'm glad you found your necklace. I know you'd been missing it quite a lot." She had taken it. Damn. And she wasn't very good at hiding her guilt. Isaac was actually a little surprised at how bad she was. It wouldn't have taken someone as good as him to see that she'd been lying and was pissed as hell the necklace was back.

"So you don't know anything about its disappearance?" Marigold raised her eyebrows. "Is that what you're trying to say?"

"Actually," Kitty said. "I do."

Isaac could practically see her thinking on her feet. He couldn't wait to hear what crap she came up with. "I found it in a pawn shop down in the city. They said a young guy had brought it in. Black hair. Pale skin. Ring a bell?" Kitty glared at Isaac. "I bought it and planned to give it to you tonight but I just hadn't had the chance yet."

"A pawn shop?" Isaac glared back. "If you're going to lie about me, please make it better than that. You think I'd steal my grandmother's jewelry and hock it at a pawn shop?" That wasn't even a good story.

Kitty shrugged. "I figured you didn't have a very good background, so you wouldn't know how to act once you got somewhere where people were taking care of you. Maybe you're worried about not having money in the future? I thought I'd buy it and then return it to Marigold's room so nobody would get in trouble."

"Didn't you say you were going to give it to me?"

"W-well." Kitty stumbled. "That's what I meant. Put it back in your room."

"That's wonderful, Kitty. I can't thank you enough for returning my necklace, no matter what the circumstances would've been. Can you give me the receipt for it, and so I can pay you back?" Marigold asked.

No way. She's not buying Kitty's shit, is she? Isaac wanted to scream.

"Oh, that's fine. Don't worry about it. I just wanted to take care of it for you." Kitty looked a little panicked.

"No, really. I'd like to see the receipt." Marigold chuckled. "I'm curious about how much a pawn shop thought this necklace was worth. Probably far less than it is."

Oh. She didn't buy it. Marigold was busily backing Kitty into a corner. Isaac suddenly had a lot of respect for the old woman.

"I...."

"You don't have one, do you?"

"Let me just look through my stuff."

"Why don't we not waste any more of our time? You stole this necklace." Marigold gave Kitty a long stare. "I know when I'm being lied to, and you, my dear, aren't even very good at it. Please clear out your desk and leave."

"You're firing me? Because your grandson is a thief. I can prove it! He might not even be your grandson. Did you ever think about that?"

"I suggest you clear out your desk now. And leave. *Now.*" Marigold hadn't ever looked so scary. Isaac wanted to do what she'd said even though she wasn't talking to him. He couldn't believe it had worked. Kitty was leaving.

"You're such a fraud," Kitty spat at Isaac. "I don't know how you pulled it off, but there's no way you're Isaac Shelley. Isaac Shelley is dead. He's been dead for years."

It hurt when she said that. Something in him twisted painfully when Kitty said that Isaac was dead. He tried to look her straight in the eye and not waver. "And you're a thief, Kitty. A liar and a thief. Please leave. My grandmother has asked you twice, and I don't think she wants to ask you again."

Kitty slammed things into her oversized handbag and tossed the keys onto the desk. "You'll be hearing from my lawyer."

"Please send any inquiries to the Falling River's lawyers in town. I'm sure they'll be happy to discuss matters with you. I won't be pressing charges, though. I think that's in everyone's best interest here."

Isaac didn't have time to ask his grandmother what she meant by that. He watched with a hidden smile while Kitty glared at them one last time and made a quick exit.

When she'd finally left the office, Marigold sighed in relief. "Well that was unpleasant. I'm glad it's over."

"Yes. You want to go up to the house and get some tea? Peppermint sounds nice right about now."

She nodded. "I think I can do that."

Isaac slung his arm over Marigold's shoulders and led her back up to the main house.

CHAPTER 13

"WHERE'S KITTY?" asked Mike the next day at lunch.

Isaac looked at Cary, but neither of them answered. It was Marigold's deal, not theirs. She probably should be the one to tell the rest of the staff.

"I had to let Kitty go," she said.

Gretchen hid a smile, their housekeeper didn't exactly seem upset, and Mike actually nodded. "I don't mind her being gone. I never much liked her anyway. She wasn't the easiest to work with. How are we going to find a replacement quickly enough for harvest?" That was Mike for you. Practical to the bone. No talking, just action.

"Ralph has agreed to step in and help train whoever I pick," Marigold told Mike. "I'm hopefully going to bring someone up from the current staff."

Isaac didn't say anything but he thought it. He'd love to run the vineyard, manage the advertising, meet with potential buyers, run tours. Kitty had always let things go that should've been capitalized on. Isaac wasn't an expert but even he saw areas where Falling River could be improved. She'd never followed all the avenues that could be explored, publicity wise or efficiency wise on a vineyard like Falling River. Probably because she'd spent so much time and effort trying to get Marigold to sign it over to her that she didn't spend any time falling in love with the place. That wasn't Isaac's problem at all. He'd been in love since the first time he walked onto the grounds. His problem was the fact that he didn't belong as much as he'd like to.

"I'll figure something out. We'll make harvest work," Marigold said. "I just needed to get her out of here."

Isaac could've sworn Marigold looked right at him when she said that thing about making harvest work. He took a big bite out of his roll and moved the bits of his salad around on his plate. He wasn't going to say anything at all. Volunteering to run harvest would be dumb. Volunteering to run Falling River would be even dumber.

"What are we doing this afternoon?" Mike asked. Isaac could tell he was eager to get everything settled in Kitty's absence.

"Cary has his wine authenticator coming in, right?"

"Yeah," Isaac said. He didn't want to be here for that. He didn't want to watch Cary convince Marigold her wines were fakes and he was crooked enough to buy them off her at a low price. It gave him a gross feeling in his belly at the thought of it.

Isaac couldn't look at Cary.

CARY DIDN'T know how to get out of the authentication. He wasn't going to take Marigold's wine, not after everything that had happened with Kitty and all. But he didn't know how not to move forward. He just had to make sure the wine was appraised the right way, he supposed. And then he walked off Falling River and didn't think about this crazy-ass job and the big disaster it had turned into ever again.

Except he'd think about Isaac every day. He already spent way too much time thinking about Isaac, and his kiss, and his taste, and the way he wrapped himself around Cary in bed at night when they were sleeping, the way he moaned Cary's name and laughed, and snuffled a little in his sleep. The way he still trusted Cary implicitly, even if he'd tried to protest that he didn't. Even after he'd realized everything he thought Cary was had been wrong. Isaac was good. He deserved this. Cary needed to leave his life and let him be the guy he should be. He looked down at his plate.

A warm hand slipped into his under the kitchen table. Isaac squeezed. Cary squeezed back. "I'd better go call and make sure he's on the right track. It's easy to get lost on all these back roads."

Cary looked at Isaac, whose face had twisted. He looked
unhappy. Cary willed Isaac to return his glance. *Trust me. I promise
I'm not going to do anything to hurt Marigold anymore, okay?* He
hated himself for being such a sucker. He hated himself for being
cynical enough to hate himself. Damn, that didn't make any sense.

Isaac pulled his hand out of Cary's grip. "I'm going to take a
dip. Today is really hot. Marigold, would you like to join me out in
the pool? We can go inside in time for the appraisal if you'd like."

"That sounds fantastic, dear."

"I'm about to head back to the vineyard, then," Mike said.

Gretchen also nodded and stood.

"I'll see you at dinner, or are you going home?" she asked.

"The wife is making pot roast tonight. I can't miss that. It's my
favorite. Plus, as soon as harvest starts, we're not going to see each
other for a month."

"You'll have to bring her and the kids over for a barbecue
soon. I can't believe we've let all summer go by, and they haven't
been here," Marigold said.

"You've been busy," Mike reminded her gently. He leaned
over and kissed Marigold on the cheek. "Don't worry about it."

Marigold gave him a kiss on the cheek in return and floated off
toward her bedroom, probably to put on a swimsuit.

"I'll see you after I call the appraiser," Cary said quietly to
Isaac. He looked him in the eye until he was sure Isaac got it.

"You're canceling, aren't you?" Isaac asked quietly.

"No, he still has to come, but I'm not going through with it.
The wines will check out just fine. Don't worry."

Isaac nodded. He leaned up and kissed Cary on the cheek. "I'll
see you in a few minutes."

"THAT ALL worked out well, didn't it?" Isaac asked. He and Cary
were in the guesthouse, as usual. As much as Marigold didn't seem
to care that they spent the night in the same room, it was still a bit
awkward. They'd gone to bed only a little while before, after a long
dinner to celebrate the continued authenticity of Marigold's prized
wines, but were lying awake with the lamp on.

"Yeah. That did. The wines are fine, Kitty's gone. All is well at Falling River." Cary smiled. "I still can't believe how easy it was to get rid of Kitty. You said the scene was kind of unpleasant, but she just left?"

"Yeah, she just packed up her stuff and took off. You know, after insulting me and making sure that Marigold knew I was a fraud, and Isaac Shelley was dead."

"Seems a little too easy to be true," Cary replied.

"You really think Kitty was the Black Mamba? She gave up awfully easily. She tried to pin the thefts on me for a little bit but as soon as it wasn't working, she just took off. I would've thought she'd be a hell of a lot harder to get rid of."

Cary shrugged. "I guess part of being good is knowing when it's time to go. She couldn't win so it was time to cut her losses, maybe."

"I just don't understand her. Why would she do that and act so awful to me, and then just leave when it gets a little tough?"

Cary kissed Isaac. "I'm guessing that's one of those things that we're probably never going to find out. I think I'm okay with not knowing."

They kissed for a while. Nothing leading, just kisses. Isaac leaned into it and tried not to count them. *Ten more kisses until he tells me he's going to leave. Five.* He'd never been good at waiting, though. He needed some sort of answer other than an intangible endpoint in the sky.

"What now?" Isaac asked. "Now that the wines have been authenticated and stuff, what are you going to do? I mean, I'd love it if you and Jules—"

Cary kissed him. Hard. Isaac figured he didn't want to talk about what he and Jules were going to do. That it probably involved moving back to Portland and forgetting this sleepy corner of California and Isaac ever existed. Isaac figured he'd better get on with his show as well. Get Marigold to sign over the trust and skip off into his own lonely sunset. But he didn't want to say good-bye yet. Or ever, really.

"Can we talk about tomorrow when tomorrow comes? I can't really hang around here. I don't think Marigold is in the habit of putting up random insurance guys for no reason. But I...." He looked like he didn't know what to say. Isaac had a sneaking feeling Cary rarely talked about his feelings. Just a thought. He smiled and let it go.

"Sure. When tomorrow comes." *For now I'll be happy with your touches. As long as they last.* Cary kissed him slowly but deeply. Isaac tried not to read it as good-bye.

"Hey," he said quietly. "I'm not trying to pressure you. I was just asking. I know technically the job is over. You didn't get what you wanted, but we're all alive and not in jail, which I think, given who we were dealing with, is probably a good thing. I just want to see you again. Maybe." Isaac buried his face in Cary's neck. He wanted to see him again a lot more than maybe. And a lot more than every once in a while. Like always.

"I'm not so complacent about it. Like, she's gone now, but who's to say she always will be? Now that both of us are on her shit list, I think I'm going to have to take her down. I doubt she's going to walk away from this and shrug it off for good. I have a feeling that neither one of us have seen the last of Miss Kitty Black Mamba."

Isaac thought Cary was probably right. "Fantastic. I'd have missed her if she was gone forever."

Cary snorted. "Right? Keep us on our toes. How long are you going to stay here?" Isaac had told him more than once he wasn't going to stay forever, assume the role of Isaac Shelley and live his life. More often than not, he wished he could but... well, he'd gone over the reasons more than once.

He shrugged. "As long as it takes, I guess. When I get the trust, I'll pay you back for the wine you had to buy. That was technically my fault anyway since I was the one being framed for the thefts. Then at least you'll be empty-handed but not in the hole too much."

"Sounds fair. Maybe I don't want your payment in money, though." Cary bit lightly at Isaac's neck.

"Are you saying you might want to see me after this?" Isaac smiled coyly.

"I might be."

Isaac did a little happy dance in his head. He tried not to let Cary see his grin.

"Well, in that case." Isaac slid a thigh over Cary's hips. "Maybe I'll hold onto the payment for a little while."

Isaac had never been very good at flirty banter—felt like a huge dork trying to do it to be honest—but there was something about the way they were when they were together that made him not care. He liked how it felt. He liked Cary. Shock of the century, right? Stop the presses. As if Isaac hadn't figured out already that he liked Cary. He just hadn't figured how much he really wanted more of Cary until the clock was ticking down to the last moments. Isaac wanted them to be something. Something to last.

Shit. Quit being a baby.

People like them didn't last. The grifter couple, Bonnie and Clyde-ing all over the country, scamming rich people from their money and making love on the go? Right. That would make a great movie, but it was a little ridiculous.

"Hey. Stop it." Cary kissed at Isaac's frown. "What's the matter?"

"Nothing. Just thinking about things."

"Can you think about how much you want to kiss me?" Cary asked. He smiled and tugged on Cary's sandy blond hair. Isaac replied with a kiss. It seemed like nearly anything they did was followed by a kiss. Maybe they were both trying to get in as many as they could before it was too late.

"I'm going to miss pulling your hair," Isaac said. "It's fun."

"That's pretty tame for you," Cary teased. Isaac blushed when he thought of half the stuff he'd said to Cary in the heat of the moment. It was so not him. At least he would've thought it wasn't. Apparently that part of him was in there, brought out by one sandy-haired commitment-phobic grifter. "I'm going to miss you pulling my hair too. For the record. But maybe you'll get to do it. You know, when you pay me back for the wine."

"Whenever that is. Who knows how long it'll take to get those papers signed. Maybe by the time I'm thirty."

"Well, I'll make sure you know how to find me," Cary said. "You know, when you're thirty."

That wasn't much in the way of commitment. Isaac would've liked a phone number, a plane ticket, a promise to stay right where he was. Maybe Cary wanted it too, and he just didn't know how to say. Wishful thinking.

"Hey again. This is supposed to be a fun night. Kitty's gone. You don't have any more problems."

"I know." Isaac forced a smile. He kissed Cary, with more force behind it. They'd always been good at kissing, even when everything else was a mess. Their kisses had left him breathless and melty since day one, but there was something different about them that night. More permanent somehow. More real. That part wasn't wishful thinking. He felt it all the way to his bones.

"I like this," Cary murmured. "I always did even when I was trying to tell myself it was all professional between you and me." He brushed Isaac's hair off his face. "Just so you know. It was never only about work between us. Never."

"Well, I've never kissed anyone who's as good at it as you are."

"I should hope not." Cary smiled, but he looked a little jealous. Isaac liked that he looked jealous, which wasn't very nice of him probably, but there you go. It was the truth.

"I haven't ever kissed anyone who was as good at it as you are either," Cary admitted.

That also felt really damn good. Isaac had hated it when he thought he was the only one affected by their kisses. He bit gently at Cary's lower lip, and then he wound their legs tighter together and pulled Cary on top of him. Time for talking was over. It was kissing time. He didn't know how many more chances he'd get to kiss Cary. Isaac ran his fingers down Cary's back and into the loose sweats he'd been lounging around in. His ass was perfect, as usual. Round muscled, a little soft. Isaac grabbed and squeezed.

CARY FELT like every touch was a good-bye, and he hated it. He honestly hated it. When he cupped his hands around Isaac's face, he wanted to do it again in the morning, and the next night. And the night after that. When Isaac mumbled in his sleep and mushed his face up against Cary's neck, he wanted to hold that moment in and never let it go. For the first time in his life, Cary wasn't happy to walk away from someone, and he didn't know what to do about it.

He lifted his hips and let Isaac push his sweats down until he was completely bare, spread across the dark duvet. Isaac stripped down too, and lifted the covers so they could wriggle their way under them. It felt good in their little cocoon of blankets, like they could touch but not look, feel without thinking so much about it. Isaac kissed him then, and pulled Cary's thigh over his hips.

"So good at this," he murmured against Cary's lips. "I love the way you kiss me." His words weren't dirty like they usually were. Cary didn't know what to do with the gentle words when he was used to it the other way.

"I love kissing you," he replied. He didn't even sound like himself. More like a love-drunk soft version of who he used to be. He didn't even mind.

Isaac drew the blankets down and trailed his fingers over Cary's chest, like he was memorizing it by the inch. He scooted down and did the same with his mouth, tasting the skin, sucking on Cary's nipples, languid, gentle. Unhurried.

Cary shuddered and dragged at Isaac's hair, trying to get him to do more. He didn't know how long he could take the heavy sweetness without making it hot and hard and fast. It was gathering in his chest and pulling painfully at his heart.

"I want you," he whispered.

"I'm getting there," Isaac said. "Look at you. Your skin is so pretty, I want to do this for hours."

Cary thought he might lose his mind if Isaac did it for one more minute. He pulled him up for what he thought would be a hard, punishing kiss, but Isaac gentled it and made it deep and dark and soft, like everything else that night. He rolled Cary onto his back.

"Want my mouth?" he asked quietly.

Good. Now it's getting to territory I recognize. Cary nodded, and Isaac smiled.

Instead of fun and quick and dirty, he went back to the teasing kisses and the swirly, light touches.

"Are you going to tease me forever?" Cary asked.

"Maybe." Isaac grinned. "I'm not doing anything better."

He took pity on Cary then, and licked a fairly direct stripe down to his straining cock. He'd have thought he wouldn't get so insanely turned on by a few kisses and some nipple play. He wasn't a kid anymore. Not even close. But he'd been waiting for Isaac's touch for ages, and he wanted it. He needed it.

Isaac wrapped his hand around Cary's cock and took one long, appreciative lick at the crown.

"You're gorgeous," he said, not for the first time. "I love the way you feel in my mouth."

His voice made Cary shiver. He thought it might have been possible for Isaac's voice alone to make him come. But his mouth? His pillowy, wet, heavenly mouth? That was going to have Cary on the edge in no time at all. He used it like he knew exactly what Cary wanted. Where he liked pressure, where he liked to be kissed. Until Isaac had Cary arching up and writhing and begging for more.

"What do you want? How do you want to come?" he asked quietly when he lifted his head.

"You. However. I don't care."

"I can do that."

Isaac sat up and reached for the bedside drawer. He pulled out what they needed. Cary was surprised when the condom was rolled down on him and Isaac slicked him up with lube. He had to grit his teeth and try not to lose control completely at the hot, slick glide of Isaac's hand. Even more, when Isaac straddled him and sank down slowly until Cary was completely inside.

They went back to slow, gliding movements. Isaac rolled his hips and twined his fingers with Cary's. It was all the heat with none of the desperation. Only closeness. Cary kept Isaac's pace the whole time, kissing his face and lips and neck until he felt Isaac's body start to clench around his.

"Are you close?" he asked.

He got a breathless "Yes," in return.

Cary cupped Isaac's jaw in one hand, and used his other to bring him to shuddering, moaning completion. It only took two more strokes for Cary to join him.

Later, when they were cleaned up and lying in the guesthouse bed, Cary made a choice. The longer he drew this out, the worse it would get. He'd want to spend more and more time with Isaac, and his real life would slip through the cracks. Cary's heart raced at the thought of losing himself to something like that. As much as so many parts of him wanted to, he couldn't hang around forever. No, it was time to cut the strings.

He had to go. Tomorrow.

CHAPTER 14

"HA-HA, DID you see that one vine? It had massive grapes on it," Isaac joked. He and Cary were coming in from a quick survey of the vineyard, on what was ostensibly Cary's last morning. They'd been helping Ralph all morning, since he'd come in last-minute, taking over for Kitty. Well, Isaac had been helping. Cary had been nothing but a distraction. Isaac was happy to have it, though, if Cary was really leaving that afternoon, like he'd announced at breakfast.

He'd been trying to have fun with him, ignore the fact that every minute was a countdown to the moment when Cary's rental car pulled out of the long driveway for good. There'd already been lots of cuddling in the morning, after a night full of saying good-bye.

"No kidding. That was like nuclear-experiment-gone-awry vine. There was something seriously funky going on wit—"

"Holy fuck."

The two of them froze in the kitchen doorway. There she was. Kitty. They'd thought she would be long gone, but she was standing with a gun. And the gun was pointing at Marigold's head.

"I want my spot back," she said. Her voice was gravelly, and she looked out of control.

Kitty's usual neat and orderly hair was wild, down, and barely brushed. Her eyes were red rimmed and bloodshot, but not like she'd been crying. It almost looked like she was on something. Isaac barely recognized her. She was frightening.

"Kitty, we went over this. You stole from me. I had to let you go." Marigold looked calm. Isaac didn't get it. Kitty had a gun pointed to her head. A gun and a crazy lady, and he wanted to do something about it, and Marigold was looking all serene and chilled out, explaining things in such a sweet little voice. He had to get her out of here. Kitty was fucking mental, and she could go off at any second. Especially if Marigold continued to say no to her.

Isaac went to lunge, but Cary held him back. He shook his head.

Not yet, he mouthed.

Isaac got it, even if every part of him wanted to do something. If either of them made a move, there was a good chance Kitty would shoot. Isaac couldn't be responsible for that. He'd never forgive himself.

"Kitty, you're going to have to let Marigold go," Cary said quietly. He gestured for Isaac to back away. He seemed to make her more angry.

It didn't make sense. Kitty should've cut her losses and gone. Gotten rid of them later on in whatever way she might think of. She didn't look right. She had to have gone off the rails somehow.

"There are other places," Marigold added. "I can give you a reference. I don't think Falling River is the right fit for you." She was trying to placate her. Isaac didn't think it was going to work.

"This place should be mine, damn it. I put in so much work. I belong here, not that street rat." She swung her gun at Isaac, who ducked, and then back at Marigold. "I want my spot back. And I want you to sign the vineyard over to me."

"I'm not going to do that, Kitty."

Marigold inched closer to her. Isaac wanted to shout at her to stop. She was an old woman. Kitty was far younger and had whatever strength that always seemed to come from adrenaline. Kitty was out of it. Her eyes looked wild. Marigold was about to try to get the gun out of her hand, and there was no way she was going to be able to do it. No way she could take Kitty out. She—

Marigold made her move. She whipped her hand up and quickly divested Kitty of the gun. Kitty stumbled back, and Marigold flipped the safety on.

"Firearms. So unnecessary." Marigold *tsk*ed. She kept the gun in her hand but didn't point it at anyone. "Now, Kitty. You and I need to have a talk."

"H-how did you do that?" Kitty looked lost and more than a little nuts. Her ferocity had died, like all it took was that one setback to completely deflate her.

"It's not important," Marigold said. "What's important is this. I asked nicely, and I'm going to ask again. I need you to leave, and I need you to leave now. Is that understood?"

"Yes."

"I'd rather not call the police. I don't like to send people to jail unless it's absolutely necessary." Marigold sighed. "Way too much paperwork."

Isaac was reeling. Who was this woman? Marigold stood there casually with a gun like it was nothing at all, treating looney-tunes Kitty like it was no big deal she'd just had a gun to her head. He'd never seen Marigold look so calm or in charge. It was like watching her identical twin with a completely different personality.

Kitty eyed the gun in Marigold's hand and backed slowly toward the door.

Marigold continued. "If you leave, I won't call the authorities. I'm fairly sure that's what's best for you. It probably won't be pretty if we get any of them involved, will it?"

Kitty shook her head.

"So, why don't you leave. Out the front door." She unclicked the safety. "I'll go ahead and keep this. You know. Just to be safe."

Kitty backed even more quickly toward the door.

"Oh, and Kitty?"

"Y-yes?"

"Please don't come back. I'd really like to not call the police today, and I most assuredly don't want to shoot anyone. I haven't done it in a while, and I'm pretty sure my aim is off. It'd take me a few shots to actually kill you. That would hurt."

Isaac thought he might pass out.

Kitty turned and ran.

Marigold smiled.

The kitchen crashed open, and a girl with wild curling hair came barreling in. Jules. "Boss, she's here!" she announced to the whole room.

"Jules," Cary hissed. "What are you doing here?"

Jules looked around the room at Marigold, Cary, and Isaac. "Saving you from getting shot?" she said.

Cary shook his head.

"Is someone going to tell me what's going on here?" Isaac said.

"Hello, dear," Marigold said to Jules. She looked down at the gun in her hand. She made a face and put it down gingerly. "I've never been a fan of firearms," she said, almost to herself. She walked around and picked up a placemat. She used it to pick the gun up and put it in a shopping bag. "We're going to have to get rid of this. How's a trip down to the lake sound to you boys?"

"Grandmother. Marigold. You're not answering me. How did you do that? Why didn't you look surprised to see Jules? Who are you?"

Marigold finally turned and looked at him. Isaac waited, not very patiently, for an answer. "I learned how to disarm people years ago. It's something we had to know growing up. I wasn't from the best part of town. It was rough, and my father wanted us to be protected."

"Grandmother, you took a gun out of the Black Mamba's hand. You may not know what that means, but it's a big deal. Kitty's dangerous. She's done a lot of bad things. I can't believe you just let her go."

Marigold chuckled. She didn't look confused at all. "You thought Kitty was the Black Mamba? Kitty? I don't know whether to laugh or be offended."

Cary froze. Jules froze. Isaac did as well. What the hell was Marigold trying to tell them? What was Marigold trying to say? "Kitty's not the Black Mamba?" Isaac asked. "She wasn't the one stealing that stuff and trying to set me up?"

"Oh, no. She was doing that. Poorly, I might add." Marigold rolled her eyes. "Amateur. What I'm saying is that Kitty is most certainly not the Black Mamba. She can barely manage to be herself."

He knew. Some tiny, terrified part of him already knew, but Isaac had to hear it for himself. He looked Marigold in the eye for a long time before he opened his mouth and spoke. "If Kitty isn't Black Mamba, then who is?"

Marigold gave them a slow smile. "Who do you think?"

CHAPTER 15

"NO. WHAT the fuck. No." Isaac backed away from Marigold quickly. He ran into a chair. It fell and clattered loudly in the quiet of the room. "You can't be."

"Why not?"

Poor Isaac looked like he was about to pass out. Cary didn't blame him. He and Jules were busy exchanging shocked looks as well. "You're Marigold Shelley."

"I am."

"You're Marigold and…. No fucking way."

Cary felt about as flabbergasted as Isaac looked. He watched Marigold. Her expression was as serene as always. Placid in the middle of Isaac's horror, Jules's shock and Cary's bewilderment.

"You can't be her. How is that even possible?"

"Oh, I assure you it's very possible. I wasn't always the wife of a rich man. I had to make my own way in the world. Your grandfather was very aware of my past. He didn't have a problem with it."

"But the Black Mamba has been active lately. The past few years, even."

Marigold gave them a rueful smile. "I know. It's hard to lose the taste for it." She glanced at Cary and Jules. "I'm guessing you two understand what I mean by that. I never take from anyone who has less money than me or lives within a hundred miles of here."

She giggled. "It keeps my pool of potential conquests to a minimum."

"You ran Roman out of the country." Isaac said, outraged. "Why did you do that?"

"Oh, no, dear. That was just a story. It was easier at the time. We didn't know who was watching him. Roman is a dear friend of mine. I made it possible for him to leave. If I hadn't, he'd probably be in prison by now. I'd have never done anything to hurt him."

"What the hell is going on here?" Isaac had gone sheet white, and he wavered.

"Here. Babe, you need to sit. Right now."

"I just don't get it. Why are you... why am I? What the hell is going on here?" Isaac repeated. He seriously looked like he was about to pass out. He wasn't making much sense. Cary had seen the signs of shock before, and he was a little worried. Cary pushed Isaac until he sat in the chair Jules had pulled out for him.

"Why don't you ask one question at a time?" Marigold said gently.

"I guess there's only one question I need to know the answer to right now. Who the hell am I?"

"You're Isaac Shelley. The only grandson I've ever had."

"You're saying I'm really Isaac Shelley? You know for sure?"

Cary watched as Isaac worked out that she must've known he was conning her the whole time. Or at least he'd thought he was. She'd been in charge of everything in the end. That had to be hitting Isaac pretty hard.

Marigold reached out to cup Isaac's hand. He didn't notice right away, but then he drew his hand out from beneath hers. She looked hurt for a second, but then she recovered. "Yes, dear. You really are Isaac Shelley. You have been since the day you were born. I am one hundred percent certain, just like I was the day you arranged for us to meet in that café."

"But...."

"Did I know you thought you weren't? Did I know you thought this was a con? Of course. I just decided I'd sit back and wait until you figured out who you really were. I didn't think I was going to have to tell you like this."

"Fucking… why?"

"You swear a lot when you're upset." Marigold continued to smile serenely.

"And Cary?"

She looked at Cary, whose throat went dry. "Oh." She chuckled. "The Nine Sisters? I know that game too. I probably know all of them, since I'm older than the dirt our vines are planted in. You put on a good show, sweetheart. Don't feel bad. I kept my eye on you at first, but you're not here for the wine anymore, are you? You're here for Isaac. As soon as I saw that, I knew I could trust you with my boy."

"And if you didn't?"

She shrugged. "I'm sure you can guess that I have my resources. You could leave, like Kitty chose to, or I could, well, make you disappear."

"You'd have killed him?" Isaac looked like he was teetering on the edge of throwing up.

"I don't do that kind of thing, no matter what I told Kitty. That's for other people. I'd have made sure he couldn't work anymore. That's probably worse for someone like Cary."

He couldn't believe how calmly she stood there talking. Or how easily she could've gotten rid of him. But she wasn't going to. Because… fuck. Because of how much he cared about Isaac. She was right. He wasn't there for any other reason.

"I don't know what to think about all of this."

"Darling, nothing's any different than it was this morning."

"Everything is different."

"No. It's not. Other than Kitty is gone, Jules has finally made her entrance—it's lovely to finally meet you in person, dear, after all those months of watching each other online, by the way. You're safe. Cary is safe, my wine is safe." She glared laughingly at Cary. "Everything is exactly as it was."

"I can't believe this." Isaac stood again, wavered for a moment, then raked the hair off of his forehead. "I need to get out of here."

Marigold's calm facade slipped at that moment. She looked horrified at the idea of Isaac leaving. "Where would you go?"

"I, just need to take a walk. Around the grounds. Alone," he said when Cary started to follow him.

"Are you sure you don't want anyone for company?" Cary asked.

"Oh, I'm sure. I think I need to think about some things for a while. I'll be back later. Don't follow me. None of you."

"We won't, dear," Marigold said.

Isaac walked out the kitchen door, and Cary and Marigold sank back into their chairs. Cary watched Marigold warily.

"Can I offer you some tea?" she asked Cary and Jules.

For some reason, that struck Cary right in the gut. He started laughing and couldn't stop. Marigold, the Black Mamba, his unfortunate state of halfway in love and halfway too damn scared to do anything about his feelings, all of it. It was too much to take, and all he could do was laugh. Marigold stared at him for a few short seconds before joining him.

Jules did what she did best: watched and rolled her eyes. Then she shrugged and wandered out to the pool without another glance at Cary and Marigold.

When they were finished laughing, Cary simply shook his head.

"That was... enlightening," he said. "I can't believe I'm in the room with you. That I've been with you for days and I had no idea."

"That's kind of the idea. Nobody is supposed to know who I am. Since my husband died, Roman is the only one. Now there are four." She glanced out the window. "I was worried how he'd take it. I guess I was right to be worried."

"I wouldn't say that. He'll be back. He just needs a few minutes to process." Cary put his hand on Marigold's arm. "I've seen the way he looks at you. He loved you even when he thought that he was faking the connection between you two. Isaac isn't going to leave for good. There's more of a chance that he'll stay now than there was before."

She sighed. "I hope so. It's been such a long time I've wanted him back in my life. I just had to wait until it was right. Until he was old enough to understand everything."

"Can I ask you a question?" Cary asked.

"Of course."

"How'd you know it was him? How are you so sure?"

Marigold smiled. "Just like you'd recognize someone from your own family, I'd have known it was Isaac anywhere." She smiled. "But there are other things."

"Like what?"

"Well." She cleared her throat. "I'm assuming you've seen his birthmark? Heart-shaped, right on the lower part of his hip?"

Cary had spent long minutes sucking on it the night before. He hoped his face didn't turn too red. "Yes. I've seen it."

"He's had that his whole life. I remember how it used to stick out of the top of his diapers when he was a baby."

"O-oh. Have you told him that?"

"No. But I will. And the way he holds his head when he has a question about something? It's just like his dad." She smiled. "And the way he looks at you. He looks just like his mother sometimes, when she looked at my Brian. It's uncanny."

"So you're sure it's him."

"Beyond sure. Yes. There was never a moment of doubt in my mind."

"I don't understand. You knew Roman had him. It's been a few years that he's been with him, right?"

"I hired Roman to find him after we were certain his remains weren't at the crash site with his parents. He owed me a friendly favor, and he's the best. No offense."

"None taken."

"It took him a while, but he's the reason I have Isaac in my life again."

"And you wanted Roman to keep him? Why, if you were so desperate to have your family back?"

"I was around. I watched Isaac from afar for all those years, watched him grow into a man, let Roman train him so that he'd understand, well, us."

"Understand that his grandmother was the Black Mamba." Cary chuckled. "That's a tall order, Marigold. And you helped his best friend disappear. He's not so happy about that either."

"Roman was ready to retire. He couldn't do it safely here. The authorities were always too close to finding him."

"But they're not after you?"

"They don't have a clue who I am. And they have no way of proving it."

"Speaking of proving it. I have your Picasso."

"Ah, yes. I'll be wanting that back. I'm glad that pushed you and Isaac to reconcile. I figured you two needed a common enemy so you could get over your little spat. I figured you'd go after the Black Mamba. I'm a little insulted you thought I was Kitty. Kitty, of all people." Marigold scoffed.

"Sorry about that."

"At least my plan worked."

"Um, we reconciled on our own before the painting came." Cary flushed. "Apparently Isaac and I are incapable of staying away from each other."

Marigold smiled one of her satisfied smiles. "I hope that stays the same."

Cary nodded. "You know what? Me too."

THEY SAT quietly for a long time that afternoon, sipping drinks, talking occasionally, and staring out at the rolling Sonoma hills. They were hazy in the late-summer warmth, lit with that golden peachy glow that only seemed to grow as the sun dipped behind the hills. Cary felt a weird sensation out there on the pool deck with Marigold, something he wasn't accustomed to. Contentment. He knew Isaac would be back eventually, after he walked off his anger. He knew Isaac and his grandmother would be fine. And he felt like he belonged there. Jules had wandered down to the vineyard to see how Mike ran things; he and Marigold had spent an hour or so getting to know each other for real. Everyone had their place. It was a very strange feeling after all.

Cary lay back and closed his eyes, let the sun hit his face, and thought about all the stuff that had gone down with this job. He didn't have his wines, but he had Isaac. He had the new addition of Marigold, and he still had Jules. He didn't know what was going to happen after Isaac came back and he and Marigold found a way to be the family they were supposed to be. He knew that things weren't going to be the same for him anymore.

He couldn't imagine going back to Portland and pretending Falling River and the people on it didn't exist.

Cary heard a splashing in the pool. He looked up to see Jules dangling her feet in the water.

"Hey, boss." Jules smiled. She looked like she'd been out in the sun for hours. Her warm caramel skin glowed, and she looked happy for once. Not content, not interested in whatever scheme they were in the middle of. Happy. It was nice to see.

"Have fun?"

"Yeah. Anything happen here while we were gone?"

Cary and Marigold looked at each other and burst into laughter. "I think we've had a pretty low-key afternoon," Cary said.

"Why do I feel like I'm missing something?" Jules asked.

"I'll fill you in on it later. Nothing big, just a lot of talking. Right now, it's time for sunbathing and iced tea."

Jules gave him a quizzical look and then leaned back in the sun. Cary knew she'd have twice as many freckles the next day, and her hair would have golden highlights in it by the end of harvest. And he also knew if Isaac wanted him, he'd still be here. Maybe not forever, maybe not all the time, but he didn't want to leave.

And he was okay with that.

ISAAC STOOD at the railing of the pool deck and watched the sun rise over the rows and rows of grapes of the Falling River vineyard. It was technically his. All of it. He couldn't believe everything that had happened the day before. When he started to think about it, his brain didn't compute.

He was really Isaac Shelley. He didn't know what to think about that. Or what to do. Everything was a huge jumble in his head. He was *Isaac Shelley*. It was harder to convince himself of that now than it had been when he was totally sure that he wasn't.

He had an identity. A real name. A family.

Then, of course, there was his family. His grandmother—well, step-grandmother, but in every way that counted, she was his family. And a famous con artist. It was almost funny that he'd come from a long line of people who didn't have much appreciation for the law. That he, well, that he was falling in love with one of them too. It made sense they'd work out together.

Isaac looked in the window of the guesthouse where Cary had fallen asleep after the long night they'd all had talking and sorting things out. The sheets were low on his golden hips, and his arms were wrapped around his pillow, mouth slightly open, hair in a messy, sandy stack on top of his head. Yeah. Isaac could easily see keeping Cary. Forever. At least that's where he hoped things were headed.

He heard shuffling, and the kitchen door opened.

"Morning, Grandmother," he said. He smiled and waved at her.

"Where's Cary?"

"Still asleep. Yesterday was a really long day."

Marigold smiled. "It was. So, have you decided on any plans?"

"For today?"

She shrugged delicately. "In general." He could tell she wasn't trying to look too hopeful. He could also tell she wanted him to stay. Isaac was having a really hard time coming up with a reason to go. She was his family. This place was supposed to be home.

"I don't know. I'm still processing things. I really love it here. It's felt like home the whole time."

"But?"

Isaac looked into the guesthouse.

"Of course. I do understand that. It hasn't been that long since I felt all of that myself."

Isaac closed his eyes for a moment and let the sun warm through his lids. "I'm not stupid. I know we're new, and I won't change my whole life around for something that might only be temporary."

"You don't feel that way about him."

"I don't. I just—"

"He doesn't feel that way about you, either. Ask him to stay, Isaac. I think you'll be surprised at what his answer is. Jules is welcome too. I think that girl and I have a lot to talk about."

Isaac knew when his Grandmother liked someone; he could see it in her eyes. He should've known she'd like Jules. Jules, who was happily sleeping in one of the house's well-appointed guest rooms. Isaac had a feeling if he asked her to stay, she wouldn't object. At least for a little while.

"I don't think I can ask them to change who they are."

"I wouldn't ask them to either. Why would they?"

But him. He needed the change. "I'm not sure I'm cut out for what you guys do, though. I'm a horrible liar."

"Isaac, you can be whoever you want to be. I'm just happy to have you back."

"I wouldn't mind taking over Kitty's work. I have a lot of learning to do, but Mike can help me out. And you."

"If that's something you'd like to do, I'd be more than happy to help you in that."

Isaac felt it right away. It was right, him and the vineyard. He'd never been all that good at the con game. He'd mostly tried to make Roman happy. He had only ever wanted a family, and now that he had one, his own family back, there was no reason to throw it away. His grandmother wasn't young. Why would he leave when he didn't have to?

"Yes. That's what I'd like to do."

"And what are you going to say to Cary?"

"Maybe...." Isaac felt a little stupid asking, but he didn't think he could do it on his own. "Maybe you can invite them to stay. It'll be less pressure than if I did. I don't think either one of them have many ties. I don't want to overwhelm them."

"I understand." She cupped Isaac's chin. "I do think that you're wrong about that, though. Cary wants to be with you. I'll be happy to give him the chance to say yes, though."

Isaac hugged his grandmother hard. "I'm going to go back inside. I'll see you at breakfast in an hour or so?"

"Yes. That sounds great. I think I'll ask Gretchen to push it back. We all had a big day yesterday. How about two hours?"

"Even better."

Two hours later, Isaac, Marigold, Cary, and Jules were gathered around the breakfast table, chatting. The others had come and gone long before. Isaac liked it that way, with just a few of them.

Marigold cleared her throat. It was time. "Cary and Jules. I know you have a base in Portland. I just wanted to make sure you knew there was always a place for you here, as well." Cary looked shocked. Jules face was a study in happy awe.

"Are you serious?" she said.

"Yes. I think, well I think this could be good for you two. Somewhere to come when you're not off conquering the world, one slightly unintelligent rich person at a time."

"I think that's a lovely offer, Marigold."

Isaac's stomach sank. Then he saw the way Cary was looking at him. Like the way Isaac thought he probably looked at Cary too, like he was something important. Like someone he wanted to have more time with. "And if it's really okay with you, I'd love to spend more time here. But Jules and I do have work to do. I can only hope you're not… opposed to it."

Marigold chuckled. "Of course I'm not. It is a bit of a family tradition, after all."

LATER THAT night, Isaac was folding some of his clothes into a duffel bag to take down to the guesthouse, which had become his unofficial room as well. He found a slip of paper in with his shirts. He didn't remember putting it there earlier. Isaac picked up the paper and unfolded it. On it was a short note written in handwriting he'd recognize anywhere.

Keep safe. Enjoy your family. I'll never be too far away.—R

Isaac smiled. That was the kind of advice he'd be happy to take.

M.J. O'SHEA grew up and still lives in sunny Washington state, and while she loves to visit other places, she can't imagine calling anywhere else home. M.J. spent her childhood writing stories. Sometime in her early teens, the stories turned to romance. Most of those stories were about her, her friends, and their favorite cute TV stars. She hopes she's come a long way since then....

When M.J.'s not writing, she loves to play the piano and cook and paint pictures, and, of course, read. She likes sparkly girly girl things, owns at least twenty different colored headbands, and she has two dogs who sit with her when she writes. Sometimes her dog comes up with the best ideas for stories... when she's not busy napping.

Visit M.J. at http://mjoshea.com. E-mail her at mjosheaseattle@gmail.com or follow her on Twitter.

Coming Home

Rock Bay: Book 1

By M.J. O'Shea

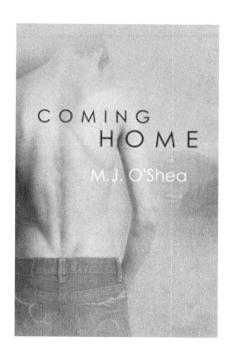

Tallis Carrington ruled Rock Bay with his gang of jocks and an iron fist—until a scandal destroyed his family's name. Ten years later Tallis is dead broke, newly homeless, and on the walk of shame to end all walks of shame. He needs money and needs it fast, and Rock Bay is the only home he knows. But the people of Rock Bay haven't forgotten him—or the spoiled brat he used to be.

The only person in town willing to overlook his past is Lex, the new coffee shop owner, who offers Tally a job even though he appears to despise Tally based on his reputation alone. When Tally discovers his gorgeous boss is the kid he tortured back in high school, Lex's hot and cold routine finally makes sense. Now Tally has to pull out all the stops to prove he was never really the jerk he seemed to be. After all, if he can win Lex's heart, the rest of the town should be a piece of coffee cake.

http://www.dreamspinnerpress.com

Letting Go

Rock Bay: Book 2

By M.J. O'Shea

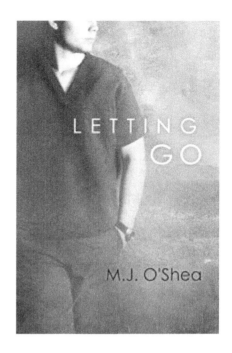

Drew McAuliffe has lived in the small town of Rock Bay most of his adult life. He'd like to be happy, but not at the cost of having his private life under his nosy neighbors' microscope, so he keeps his bisexuality under wraps.

After a messy breakup that caused him to pack up and move to Astoria, on the Oregon coast, Mason Anderson decides to avoid drama of the romantic kind. All he wants is to start over—alone.

But Drew and Mason were meant to meet. The long looks and awkward half hellos chance offered were never going to be enough. But when they do finally come together on the worst night possible, misconceptions and problems from their pasts get in the way. Until Mason learns to trust again—and until Drew learns to let go of who he thinks he is—a real connection is nothing but a pipe dream.

http://www.dreamspinnerpress.com

Finding Shelter

Rock Bay: Book 3

By M.J. O'Shea

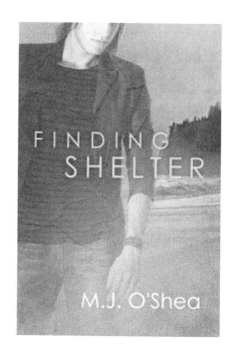

Justin Foster has nineteen years of nothing but trouble behind him. After escaping his abusive father, he finds himself in Rock Bay, Washington, with his cousin Travis. Justin is bruised and has a hard time trusting, but with the help of his family and the small town, he might be able to heal.

Logan O'Brien is also new in town, hoping he can finally get away from his past and the memories of the girlfriend who shattered his heart. It doesn't take him long to realize Rock Bay can be more than safe harbor: it can also be home. And for the first time in his life, he finds himself captivated by a man—by Justin.

Justin is attracted to Logan too, but he's also wary. Physically, Logan reminds him a bit too much of the closeted jerks who used to beat him up after school. But after one awkwardly amazing kiss, he's smitten, despite how his past and insecurities continue to haunt him. Logan's love, faith, and stubbornness are just what Justin needs to believe their love is worth fighting for.

http://www.dreamspinnerpress.com

Newton's Laws of Attraction

By M.J. O'Shea

Rory was Ben's oldest and best friend until senior year of high school, when they confessed they'd harbored feelings for each other all along. They enjoyed only a few months of happiness until Ben chose closeted popularity over true love… and he's regretted it ever since.

Eight years later, Ben is out and proud and teaching art at the same high school he graduated from. When he learns the chemistry teacher is retiring, he's excited to meet her replacement until he finds out the brand new teacher is none other than Rory Newton—the first love he's never quite gotten over. Despite a painfully awkward start, it doesn't take Ben long to realize he'll do whatever it takes to win Rory back. But it's starting to look like even his best might not be enough.

http://www.dreamspinnerpress.com

Impractical Magic

By M.J. O'Shea

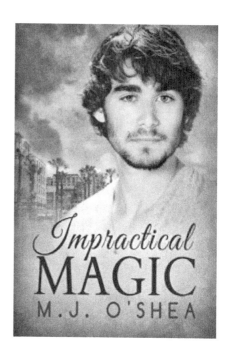

Physics teacher Fenton Keene is looking forward to a summer of doing nothing but hanging out with friends and maybe getting into a little trouble. With his best friend out of town, trouble seems like the best option and it comes in the form of his building's newest temporary resident, a gorgeous fireman named Kevin.

Fen's been attracted to men before, but this is the first time he's considered acting on it. And act he does.

Fen and Kevin have an intense summer fling. Just in time for Kevin to go home, more feelings develop than Fen can ignore, but they don't stop Kevin from leaving. Once Kevin's gone, Fen can't stop thinking about him. That's when reality sets in and Fen faces the difficulties of distance and fidelity, while Kevin balks at Fen's reluctance to tell his friends and family. They just need to find a way to make their magic more practical.

http://www.dreamspinnerpress.com

Moonlight Becomes You

Lucky Moon: Book 1

By M.J. O'Shea and Piper Vaughn

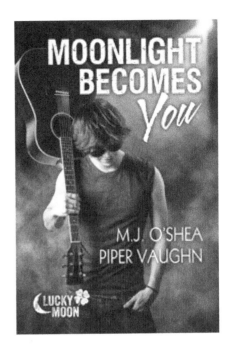

Eleven years ago, Shane Ventura made the biggest mistake of his life when he caved in to pressure from his record label to kick his best friend, Jesse Seider, out of their band, Luck. To this day, Shane has never wanted anyone more, and all the sex and alcohol in the world can't fill the void Jesse left behind. Not even the prospect of teaming up with Britain's hottest band, Moonlight, for a massive world tour can get him out of his funk. Then he meets lead singer Kayden Berlin and falls into instant lust.

Kayden may act like he's not interested, but Shane knows he feels the spark between them. Yet the harder Shane pushes, the more Kayden pulls away, until one explosive night leaves Shane with a broken heart. That seems to be his lot—lucky at everything but love. Shane still has one lesson left to learn, though: when it comes to love, you can't always leave things to chance.

http://www.dreamspinnerpress.com

The Luckiest

Lucky Moon: Book 2

By M.J. O'Shea and Piper Vaughn

Rock star Nick Ventura has finally hit rock bottom. Jealous of his brother's new love, he overindulges in his usual vices and winds up crashing his car into a department store in a drunken haze. Publicly humiliated and on the verge of jail time, he enters a court-ordered rehabilitation program.

Nutritionist Luka Novak is flamboyant, effeminate, and the type of gay man bisexual Nick would normally sneer at. But Luka's sunny nature hides a deep hurt caused by an unfaithful ex-boyfriend. As much as Luka knows he should be wary of Nick's reputation, he's drawn to Nick despite himself. Their tentative friendship turns into romance, but Luka soon comes to realize Nick's fear of losing his bad boy reputation means he'll probably never go public with their relationship.

Nick never needed anyone until Luka came into his life. Now he has to reconcile his carefree past with the future he suddenly wants more than anything. And the first lesson he must learn is how to become the man both he and Luka need him to be, rather than stay the boy he always was. Alone.

http://www.dreamspinnerpress.com

One Small Thing

One Thing: Book 1

By M.J. O'Shea and Piper Vaughn

"Daddy" is not a title Rue Murray wanted, but he never thought he'd have sex with a woman either. Now he's the unwitting father of a newborn named Alice. Between bartending and cosmetology school, Rue doesn't have time for babies, but he can't give her up. What Rue needs is a babysitter, and he's running out of options. He's on the verge of quitting school to watch Alice himself when he remembers his reclusive new neighbor, Erik.

Erik Van Nuys is a sci-fi novelist with anxiety issues to spare. He doesn't like people in general, and he likes babies even less. Still, with his royalties dwindling, he could use the extra cash. Reluctantly, he takes on the role of manny—and even more reluctantly, he finds himself falling for Alice and her flamboyant father.

Rue and Erik are as different as two people can be, and Alice is the unlikeliest of babies, but Rue has never been happier than when Alice and Erik are by his side. At least, not until he receives an offer that puts all his dreams within reach and he's forced to choose: the future he's always wanted, or the family he thought he never did.

http://www.dreamspinnerpress.com

One True Thing

One Thing: Book 2

By M.J. O'Shea and Piper
Vaughn

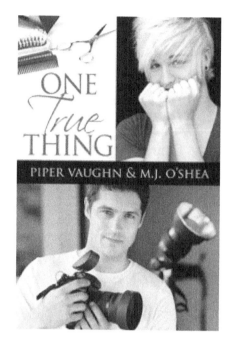

Dustin Davis spent years wishing
for a prince but kissing frog after
slimy frog. When he sees Archer Kyriakides for the first time, Dusty
thinks his luck has finally changed. Archer could be it. The One. But
their hot and cold romance leaves Dusty confused: why does it feel
right one moment and wrong the next? It doesn't make sense—until
the day Dusty meets Archer's identical twin, Asher, and realizes
he's been seeing them both.

Asher Kyriakides dreams of being a fashion photographer, but he's
stuck with a job he hates and an irresponsible playboy brother whose
habits drive him absolutely insane, especially when he finds out
Archer is dating the cute little blond Asher can't seem to forget.
Torn between loyalty and desire, Asher does nothing but try to warn
Dusty away.

But when Archer finally goes too far, Dusty turns to Asher for
comfort, and Asher knows he can't refuse. It isn't long before they
realize they're falling fast, but more than one thing stands in their
way, not the least of which is Archer, who isn't quite ready to stop
being a thorn in his brother's side.

http://www.dreamspinnerpress.com

Catch my Breath

By M.J. O'Shea

Danny Bright was born to entertain. He just needs his big break. So when he hears that Blue Horizon Records is holding auditions looking for the next big thing, Danny jumps at the chance. It doesn't turn out exactly as he imagined, though. Instead of getting solo contracts, Danny and four other guys are put into a boy band.

Innocent, idealistic Elliot Price thinks he's headed for college. An impulsive decision to sing in the local talent search changes all that. A bigwig producer happens to see him, hands him a business card, and turns Elliot's life upside down.

Elliot and Danny are close from the beginning. They love all the guys, but it's different with each other. Soon their friendship turns into feelings more intense than either of them can ignore. The other three boys only want Danny and Elliot to be happy, but when their management team and record label discover two of their biggest tween heartthrobs are in a relationship, they're less than pleased. Danny and Elliot find themselves in the middle of a circle of lies and cover-ups, all with one bottom line—money. They have to stay strong and stick together if they don't want to lose themselves… and each other.

http://www.dreamspinnerpress.com

Macarons at Midnight

By M.J. O'Shea and Anna Martin

M.J. O'Shea • Anna Martin

Tristan Green left his small English town for Manhattan and a job at a high profile ad agency, but can't seem to find his bearings. He spends a lot of time working late at night, eating and sleeping alone, and even more time meandering around his neighborhood staring into the darkened windows of shops. One night when he's feeling really low, he wanders by a beautiful little bakery with the lights still on. The baker invites him in, and some time during that night Tristan realizes it's the first time he's really smiled in months.

Henry Livingston has always been the odd duck, the black sheep, the baker in an old money family where pedigree is everything and quirky personalities are hidden behind dry martinis and thick upper east side townhouse facades. Henry is drawn to Tristan's easy country charm, dry English wit, and everything that is so different from Henry's world.

Their new romance is all buttercream frosting and sugared violets until Tristan's need to fit in at work makes him do something he desperately wishes he could undo. Tristan has to prove to Henry that he can be trusted again before they can indulge in the sweet stuff they're both craving.

http://www.dreamspinnerpress.com

Random Acts

By Mia Kerick

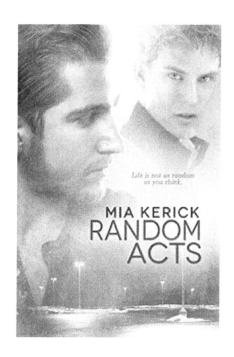

Bradley Zelder can't find his way in life. After struggling for nearly a decade, he has yet to complete his college degree. Working as a school custodian, living in blue-collar Landsbury, MA, his love life is as empty as the rest of his existence. But on his way home after another disastrous date, his truck breaks down in upscale Oceanside. When he thinks life can't get any worse, a man who is the epitome of Boston elite and everything Bradley finds attractive and intimidating helps him move his truck to the side of the road. Ashamed of his lot in life, Bradley almost lets the opportunity slip away, but he comes to his senses in time and tracks Caleb down.

From a random act of kindness, romance begins to grow, filling all the dark corners of Bradley's empty life—until a random act of violence threatens to take it all away. Bradley must step up and be the man Caleb believes him to be. Caleb rescued him from a life without hope. Can Bradley rescue him in return?

http://www.dreamspinnerpress.com

THE GENERAL AND THE ELEPHANT CLOCK OF AL-JAZARI

SARAH BLACK

http://www.dreamspinnerpress.com

WE DANCED

J E F F **E R N O**

http://www.dreamspinnerpress.com

CPSIA information can be obtained at www.ICGtesting.com
Printed in the USA
LVOW05s0633160115

423093LV00003B/272/P

9 781632 165251